# Deep

## A Paranormal Novel

## By
## Natavia

# Prologue

## *Atlantic Ocean 1619...*

*The smell of blood mixed with vomit, feces and urine filled the bottom of the ship. Around sixty slaves were chained by bilboes—leg shackles. Three Caucasian men with a British accent walked down the rickety stairs with pails of food. It had been days since their last meal. A young female slave, around the age of twenty, refused to eat. She gave her scraps to the pregnant woman next to her.*

*"You have to eat," the pregnant woman told Adwoa. Adwoa's ankles were infected from the rusty bilboes. She was running a fever and couldn't keep anything down because of the infection traveling through her body. Adwoa was dying.*

*"This one is dead!" a sailor yelled out.*

"Throw him over!" a sailor named John replied.

Loud screams from the dead man's wife filled the ship as they unchained him. The two sailors carried his stiff body up the stairs to throw him overboard. The third sailor checked for more bodies and found ten more, two were babies.

"We got ten more!" he yelled out to the sailors upstairs.

"Eat, Adwoa. You're going to die," the pregnant woman said. She put the food against Adwoa's mouth, but she turned away from her. Adwoa's lips were cracked and bloody from dehydration. She was frail, and it pained her to breathe.

"The water is going to take my soul, so I can be at peace. You should come with me," she said. The pregnant woman was puzzled. Why would Adwoa want her to kill herself and her baby?

"My baby is still moving inside me. We have a chance. Please, eat!" the pregnant woman cried.

"I hear her voice. She wants me to join her, so my soul could rest. The water will save your soul, too. Stop eating and drinking from them so we can be free," Adwoa said. Suddenly, the ship tilted, and the wood squealed from the force of the waves. Water seeped into the cracks of the ship until a hole appeared underneath. The sailor tried to make a run for it, to warn the others above, but he tripped. The pressure from the water slammed his body into the stairs, causing the stairs to collapse.

"She came for us," Adwoa said.

"We're going to die!" someone yelled out.

The water began filling up the bottom of the ship, drowning the slaves as they tried to break free, but they were chained. Adwoa closed her eyes, welcoming the feeling her ancestors told stories of. The spirits of the water were real, and they came to save them...

# Shore

## Present day, June 2nd, 2017...

I sat on the steps to our building waiting for my mother to come home from work. It was late at night, so I always waited outside for her because of the condition of our neighborhood. We lived in the slums where the buildings were falling apart, and the water was barely hot, but it was all she could afford. I wanted to help her, but I had a rare brain disease, so I was considered handicap. At twenty years old, I felt like a child. I had several jobs but had to quit them all because of my seizures but we didn't want social security. My mother figured my condition would change once we found the right doctor. She didn't want to believe I was permanently damaged and neither did I. My father was killed at work when I was a little girl—well, I was a newborn baby. He was a manager at a liquor warehouse. Apparently, he fired an employee, who came back two weeks later and shot my father. My mother was a young woman at the time, she was only twenty-one years old. Twenty years later, her life was still at a standstill.

"Aye, pretty lady. When are you gonna let me come up? I know Sabrina is hard up on money right now. I'll pay," a man said to me. He reeked of alcohol and his eyes were bloodshot red. His clothes were a size too small, perhaps that was the fashion for men nowadays. He was also far from attractive and old enough to be my father. His name was Lester, and he was the neighborhood pervert.

"Get the hell out of my face!"

My bluntness seemed to entice him even more. He grabbed my leg and squeezed, showing me his old gold tooth.

"I like a feisty little bitch," he grinned.

"Leave her alone before I call the cops!" Miranda yelled out the fourth-floor window. Miranda was the neighborhood's daycare lady and she hated Lester with a passion.

"Let me know when you're ready for me, pretty lady," Lester said while grabbing himself. He caressed my cheek before walking away.

"Get in the house, Shore! You know there is nothing but trouble this time of night!" Miranda said, smoking a cigarette.

"I'm not a kid," I replied.

"Your mother told me to look after you," she said, and it angered me. I had a health issue, but I was almost twenty-one years old!
"I'll be fine."

"We just care about you," Miranda said, and I smiled at her.

"Thank you."

A few seconds later, my mother's old Chevy Impala pulled into the parking lot. The car was on its last leg and it rattled terribly. My mother worked at a small diner in the inner-city of Annapolis. She depended on her tips because her pay was only two dollars and seventy-five cents an hour. My mother got out of her car and slammed the door. She had a brown paper bag in her hand which meant she stopped at the liquor store before she came home. My mother was an alcoholic which also put pressure on our situation. Sabrina was a beautiful woman despite her disheveled hair and the dark rings around her eyes. She was a curvy woman, perhaps a size twenty. Her long, jet-black hair fell to her hips and her skin was the color of cocoa bark.

"What happened?"

"That son-of-a-bitch fired me!" my mother shouted as she walked up the steps to the building. I was used to my mother losing her job. The diner was the only job she managed to keep over five months. I followed her into our small two-bedroom apartment. She sat on the couch and popped the top off her Jameson Irish Whiskey bottle. I sat across from her needing answers because the rent was almost due. The landlord gave us one last warning. If our rent was late again, we would have to move. My mother was the only child of her parents, but they were dead. I have never met my father's side of the family because my mother didn't know them.

"I need to get a job."

"Jobs stresses you out and triggers your seizures. I only have twenty damn dollars to my name because I had to get that piece of shit car fixed. We have to move. I can't come up with five-hundred dollars in a week. Just start packing and I'll figure out a way," she said.

"But, Ma, you bought liquor with the tips you made tonight?"

"Damn it, Shore! I'm trying, okay! It's not easy taking care of us! You think I don't get stressed, too?" she asked with tear-filled eyes.

"Sorry, Ma. I'll go pack. Where will we go?" I asked, feeling defeated.

"Your father's family's house. Well, his ancestors' house. He always said if something happened to him for me to take you there. I've never seen it before, but he gave me an old map. It's been abandoned for years so let's hope it's still there. If it isn't, then I guess we'll have to sleep in the car until I find something else. I'd rather just leave now before the landlord has all of our belongings outside," she said. My heart fell to the pit of my stomach at the mention of sleeping in a car. There had to be another way. I went to my shoebox bedroom and cried my eyes out. The apartment wasn't much but it was my home. We moved every year and it was draining. I was so used to it that I only kept a bed and dresser in my room. We didn't own a TV, but I had a cell-phone. The cell-phone's service was terminated but I used it for the internet. Social media was my only connection to the world and I actually had a few friends on there who were like me and didn't have a life outside of their bedroom. I learned how to style my own hair, how to put on make-up and I also knew the fashion because of the internet models. In my head, I attended one of those fancy colleges, had a circle of friends, drove a cute convertible and had a cute boyfriend. But when I opened my eyes, nothing but cracked walls and foggy windows surrounded me.

*I'm gonna find a job and help my mother. Even if it kills me!*

# Shore

**Two days later...**

"**S**hore! Do you hear me talking to you?" my mother asked. I walked around the small cabin in the woods not believing what was happening. The drive was three hours away from our apartment, but it took us four hours to find the house because it was buried behind hundreds of trees. I was excited on our way to our new home and anxious because we never lived in a house before. But the excitement went away soon as we found it.

"We can't live here. Are you sure you read the map, right? This can't be it," I replied. The small bedroom I stood in was supposed to be my bedroom and it faced the pretty blue crystal lake. Virginia didn't have pretty blue water, so I didn't understand why the water was so pure. I couldn't pull away from the dirty window because the scenery was amazing.

"This is definitely the right house. Your father's slave ancestors owned it. This house is history and you should be thankful for it," she replied.

"The lake is the only good thing about it."

"This is only temporary. At least you won't have to worry about those damn crackheads sitting on our car. Oh, and what about the gunshots in the middle of the night? This ain't much but it's ours until we get back on our feet," she said.

"I'd rather live in the hood than in the woods. You haven't seen the movie, *Cabin Fever*? Or what about *Evil Dead*? Shit happens to people in the darn woods, Ma! Do we even have electricity? This is soooooo seventeenth century."

"Cut the bullshit out, Shore! This will be our home for a while unless you have a better idea. Times are hard and even though we don't have that fancy mess you're worried about, we have each other. Just imagine we're back in our old apartment and I couldn't afford to pay the electric bill. It's not like we haven't lived this way before," she replied.

"We only have two-hundred dollars to our name and that was from selling our furniture. We're in the middle of nowhere and our car is on its last leg. How are we going to work from here? Let's just get a motel room so I can look for a job in walking distance. People live out of motels all the time."

"You have epilepsy, Shore. You shouldn't be working! I'll find a job, plus I told you not to work in the first place."

"For ten years I had to wear a helmet, Ma. I couldn't do things normal kids did and I didn't have any friends. I'm twenty years old and should be having fun, working and going out to clubs. All I do is read books and browse the internet, but I can't do that anymore since we don't have Wi-Fi out here," I replied.

"I'll worry about work, just finish unpacking." My mother kissed me on the forehead before she left out of the room. Tears fell from my eyes because deep down inside, I knew I couldn't live a normal life. My biggest fear was having a seizure that I couldn't wake from, so it was a must that I couldn't do the things I wanted.

# Shore

## Four days later...

My mother was inside the house making us sandwiches and fresh lemonade. It was humid, and we didn't have an air conditioner, but sitting by the lake gave me a slight breeze. I was sitting on a rock looking at the small fish swim around. One fish glowed, and it had colors like the rainbow.

"What kind of fish is that?" I said out loud. Looking further into the water, I saw my reflection. The lake seemed like it understood me for some reason.

*Step into the water, Shore. Our queen wants to see you,* the voices said. I could feel a seizure coming. Every time I heard voices or saw crazy images, I'd collapse then wake up in a hospital. It wearing basketball shorts and tennis shoes. The stranger also wore a gold seashell necklace around his neck which I thought was odd for a man. The guys on social media wore Jesus pieces with diamonds and many other things around their necks but not seashells.

"Do you hear me talking to you?" he asked.

"I'm sorry. What was that?"

"Never mind, you look fine to me. Can I fish here? I have been coming here for a while because I thought it was abandoned," he said. His voice oozed sexiness. Hell, everything about the man was perfect. His full lips curved into a smile when he talked. Staring into someone's face and not talking to them was rude and weird but I couldn't help it.

"Ummm, uh. I'm no—not sure," I finally replied.

*Damn it! I'm stuttering, and he probably thinks I'm crazy.*

"Okay then. I'll see you around," he said and walked away. I began feeling guilty. Besides, what did I have to lose by letting him fish at the lake?

had been happening since I was a little girl and it
had only gotten worse as I got older.

*I can't swim.*

*Yes, you can, Shore. Come swim with us.
You're home now.*

*Leave me alone!*

*It's time to come home,* the voices were
echoing in my head and made my nose bleed. I
used my shirt to stop the bleeding.

"Excuse me. Can I fish here?" a voice asked
from behind. I turned around and almost fell off
the rock. The man hurriedly rushed over and
caught me. My body got lost in his strong arms as
he held me. His scent was unusual but
nonetheless he smelled good.

"Are you okay?" he asked, staring into my
eyes. He was dark-skinned with a unique
complexion. There was an emerald tint to his skin
underneath the sunlight. His teeth were perfect
and white like flour. When he stood up, he was
extremely tall. The stranger was around six-foot-
six and he had pretty and thick curly hair that was
brushed into a ponytail. He was shirtless and only

"I'm sorry! You can fish here!" I called out to him.

"Appreciate it," he said and walked back over towards me. I noticed he didn't have fishing rods or even a bucket to keep them in.

"So, where is your stuff?" I asked, and he chuckled.

"I use my hands when I'm fishing. Do you want me to show you?" he asked. Before I could respond, my mother ran out of the house with a shotgun in her hand. I slapped my hand against my forehead because she was embarrassing me!

"Get your ass away from my daughter! This is private property!" she yelled at the stranger.

"Put the gun down," he said. My mother dropped the gun on the ground and everything that was happening from that point on was out of the ordinary. A stranger comes out of nowhere and he actually got my mother to listen without putting up a fight?

"I'm not here to cause any harm. I just want to fish for my father. Is that okay with you?" he asked.

"Yes," my mother replied.

"Are you okay, Ma?"

"Yes. I'm going to finish our lunch," she said and walked back into the house.

"Wowwwwww, I'm surprised she didn't curse you out," I said, and the stranger looked down at me.

"I'm not a threat. Sorry for my rudeness but my name is Zambezi." He extended his hand out to me and I shook it.

"I'm Shore." I couldn't stop blushing if I wanted to. Zambezi didn't seem like a city boy and I wondered if he lived close by.

"Do you live near here?" I asked.

"Very close but we don't have a lake behind our house," he said. I put my hair behind my ear and looked down at my outfit. I cursed myself out for wearing my short summer dress without any shoes. Something told me to polish my toe nails, but I didn't unpack everything yet.

"How old are you?" I asked.

"A year older than you," he chuckled.

"You don't know my age."

"Twenty," he said, and I blushed again.

"How did you guess that?"

"I'm good at guessing a lot. Do you want to watch me fish?" he replied.

"Sure, it's not like there is anything else to do."

Zambezi stepped into the lake after he took his shoes off and I sat back on the rock with my chin rested on my hand. There was something about him. I had many crushes in the past, but Zambezi was different—very different. He went inside his pocket and sprinkled something in the water.

"What is that?"

"Fish bait," he replied.

Suddenly, the fish came out of nowhere, surrounding Zambezi.

"What in the hell! Get out of the water!" I yelled at Zambezi. The way the fish surrounded him made me nervous.

"It's cool, chill out. My body temperature and the bait draw them in. The fish in this lake are different. You don't need a fishing rod to catch them. It's a whole other world here," he said. Zambezi grabbed two fish out the water and tossed them into the grass. By the time he was finished, there was a pile of big fish lying next to the rock. I'll never look at fish the same again.

"Those are old fish. Fish that were going to die anyway," he said when walked out the water.

"Your dad is going to eat all of that?" I asked.

"No, he sells them at his fish market. We don't eat fish," he said.

"What can you possibly use from a fish other than food?"

"It's a secret," he said and smiled at me. I could look at Zambezi all day and not get bored. He was easy to talk to and had a calmness to him. Most handsome guys with nice bodies seemed stuck on themselves when I was in school and even at work. He wrapped some kind of weird net around the fish and threw it over his back.

"You need help?"

"No, I'm straight. Thanks for letting me fish here. Next time, I'll knock on the door and ask," he said. Zambezi grabbed his shoes and disappeared into the woods. My mother walked outside with two plates in her hand. She sat on the rock next to me.

"What is my gun doing out here?" she asked. I stopped chewing my food and stared at her. My mother was losing it!

"Ma, you brought it out here. You were ready to shoot Zambezi."

"Who is that? And when the hell did that happen?"

"Like twenty minutes ago. He came here to fish," I said.

"Are you okay, Shore? I didn't see anyone here. Now eat your food because we have a long day ahead of us. We have to do a lot of dusting and wash those dirty windows. This place wouldn't be so bad if it was clean," she said.

"Ma, did you have a drink? There was a guy here around my age and he went fishing in the lake. He's very tall and couldn't be missed. You talked to him."

"You always hear or see things when you're ready to have a spell. I'll clean the house, so you can get some rest," she said.

*What in the fuck is happening here?* I thought.

We ate in silence until it was time for my mother to start cleaning. I went back inside the house and into my bedroom. While staring at the ceiling, I couldn't stop thinking about Zambezi. I wanted to know more about him and his unexplainable presence.

**The next day...**

"We have to do something about the tub. I don't think it's big enough for us," I complained.

"Will you stop acting like we had a very glamorous life before we moved here?" my mother replied while I dumped water into the tub from the lake. I had to boil the water in the fireplace to kill the germs. Taking a hot bath in a hundred-degree weather was overkill.

"Take your bath so we can walk to the small town nearby. We have to get a few things," my mother said before she walked out the house. The tub we had in the corner of the kitchen was a metal old fashioned tub that you could move around the house. Draining it was hard to do because me and my mother had to push it outside to let the water out. Living in the cabin was like a job itself and I was drained.

"The water is cold already!" I yelled out in frustration. It was boiling hot just a few minutes ago and suddenly it was ice cold, causing me to shiver.

"Ma, can you bring me the space heater?" I shouted out, but she didn't answer me.

"MA!" I called again but nothing.

"Damn it!"

I took a quick bath before reaching for my towel on the chair next to the tub. When I stood to step out of the tub, my legs wouldn't move.

*Nooo. God please don't let me have a seizure while in the tub. I can drown.* My mouth opened to scream for my mother, but I couldn't hear my voice. It was almost like having an out-of-body experience. I was alert, but I couldn't talk or move. Tears welled in my eyes while I frantically searched around the cabin. Something different was happening. The water inside the tub spilled out onto the floor. The inside of the cabin was no longer familiar and the furniture we had inside was replaced with old furniture—furniture that I was unfamiliar with.

"SHORE!" a voice called out.

My mother ran to me, catching me in her arms before my body hit the floor. Everything was back to normal. The water that spilled out onto the floor was back inside the tub.

"What happened? Are you okay? Answer me!" my mother's voice trembled as she held me. Tears wouldn't stop falling from my eyes because I was scared shitless. Although I couldn't explain my seizures, I knew there was something else happening to me now.

"This cabin is cursed, Ma. This place is cursed! Please take me away from here!" I panicked.

"Calm down, Shore. Just take deep breaths before you have an anxiety attack," she said.

"Just tell me you saw Zambezi yesterday. Something is wrong here!"

My mother grabbed my face and forced me to look at her. I knew that look all too well. She really had no clue of what I was talking about.

"I know this is very hard, Shore. God knows I'm gonna get us out of here but please just bear with me. Nobody is here but us and this place being cursed is a bunch of non-sense. The seizures cause you to see things that aren't there," she said.

"I'm gonna go and get dressed," I replied.

I went into my bedroom to get dressed. After I was finished, I grabbed my brush and put my hair into a wild ponytail. I used a little edge control to smooth out my edges. Afterwards, I put lip gloss on my lips. The maxi dress I was wearing was a little too snug. I had it for five years and my hips were protruding. I needed new clothes because my figure was outgrowing my old teenage clothes. My mother stood in the doorway with her arms crossed.

"Well, don't you look beautiful. I still remember the day I went into labor like it was yesterday. My baby isn't a baby anymore," she said.

"I'll always be your baby."

"Come on. Let's catch the market before it closes," she said.

My mother grabbed her basket by the door before we left out of the house. It was my first time being away from the cabin since we moved in, but my mother went to the market a few times without me. It surprised me how well she was getting familiar with the area.

"This place reminds me of back in the day. A lot of dirt roads, trees and water. It's almost like it's not a part of the world. What if this place is like a secret or something and it's a gift for us to know about it?"

My mother threw her head back in laughter, "Chile, why does your mind wander the way it does? This is just ol' country living. You have watched too many movies," she said.

The walk was almost an hour. My mother seemed happier than she's ever been. The dark circles around her eyes were almost gone and she didn't smell like liquor like she normally does. I could actually smell the sweet perfume she was wearing. Sabrina looked younger and I don't know how I missed it. Guilt pulled at my conscious. Here I was being a whiney brat and not realizing how happy my mother seemed to be.

"WOW!" I said in excitement when we walked into the town. The place was beautiful! The stores were old fashioned and there wasn't a car in sight. People were selling fresh produce and handmade jewelry at their stands alongside the street. The sounds of African drums echoed throughout the town while a few happily danced in the street.

"What is this?"

"Many, many years ago, African slaves settled here with the Native Americans. This place isn't on the map. You have to be from here to learn how to get here," she said.

"Runaway slaves came here?"

"Yes," she replied.

My mother gave a woman a quarter and she dropped four peaches into my mother's basket. No wonder my mother wasn't concerned about money, the markets were way cheaper than the city we came from.

"There is a storm coming in a few days. Make sure you stay away from the windows," the woman said to my mother. The lady that sold the peaches had pretty long silver hair that was in two braids. She had symbols on her hands that I couldn't keep my eyes off of.

"Shore, Giva is talking to you," my mother said while nudging me.

"It's okay. She's into the ink on my hands. Come back tomorrow so I can teach them to you,"

Giva said. While my mother was picking out corn, I caught a glimpse of Giva's eyes changing colors. Her once brown eyes were dark green with a tint of blue. When my mother looked up, Giva's eyes turned back to their normal color.

*Get in the water, chile. You need the lake!* Her voice came into my head. I pretended I didn't hear her. Maybe I was really losing my mind. A woman came out of the market behind Giva's stand and her beauty was remarkable. Her skin was the color of roasted chestnuts and her long locs were wrapped into a bun. She wore a dashiki dress and the gold charm bracelet she wore around her wrist reminded me of chimes as she waved her hand. When she caught me staring at her, I turned my head.

"Adwoa, this is Sabrina and her daughter, Shore. They're new to town," Giva said to the woman. She looked at me and my mother with an unwelcoming expression.

"Nice to meet you," I held my hand out to Adwoa. If looks could kill, I would've been dead.

"I know who you are. My son went fishing at your cabin yesterday," Adwoa said.

"You're Zambezi's mother?" I asked in disbelief. Adwoa looked like she was only twenty-five years old.

"I did call him my son, eh?" Adwoa replied in her heavy accent. Giva waited until Adwoa was gone before she started talking again.

"What's her problem?" my mother asked Giva.

"Adwoa doesn't like new people. Stay out of her way and she'll stay out of yours. She's also very protective over her family. So, stay away from them," Giva warned us. We thanked Giva before we walked away.

"That Adwoa woman is a bitch. I hope I don't have to kick anyone's ass," my mother whispered as we walked past a jewelry stand. We made a few more stops before we headed towards the fish market. I told my mother we had plenty of fish in the lake because I wanted to avoid running into Zambezi.

"We don't have fishing rods, and besides, who is gonna clean them?" my mother asked.

"Can we hurry up because I have to take a number two. My stomach is bubbling."

I was getting nervous and sweat beads formed on my forehead. After meeting Adwoa, I wanted no parts of Zambezi.

"We'll be in and out," she said.

The fish market was the biggest market out of the rest. They had everything! Vitamins, natural herbs, meat, fish, chicken and plenty other seafood. The market had three levels. It was the only building in the town that had a modern feel to it. My mother went over to the wine table as I looked around. A small group of females stared at me and they weren't too pleased with my presence either.

*Here we go with this bullshit. This is like high school all over again. I guess they're about to come over here to remind me that I'm a loser. Why are they dressed normal anyway? They shop at designer stores?* I thought, as the small group made their way towards me. The ring leader was tall and curvy. Her hair was bone-straight with a part in the middle. She was wearing a skirt with a half-top. Her heels clicked across the floor and I couldn't keep my eyes off her shoes. If only we could afford nice things.

"So, you're the new girl in town?" she asked.

"I guess you can say that."

"What are you wearing? I thought people on the outside had better taste in fashion. What material is this?" she asked, touching my dress. Her friends behind her giggled and cracked corny jokes. If only they knew I heard those jokes a thousand times before. I smacked her hand away and her friends stopped laughing.

"Let's just leave her alone, Laguna," one of them said.

"Did you just touch me, bitch?" Laguna, the ring leader asked.

"Don't you ever put your hands on me again. Say what you want to me but do not fuckin' touch me!"

My mother heard the commotion and rushed over. Just when I thought she was going to give up drinking, she had four jars of moonshine.

"What is going on?" my mother asked.

"Nothing, we're just getting to know each other," I replied.

"Y'all don't belong here," Laguna said before her and her posse walked away.

"I can't believe I'm almost twenty-one and still getting bullied. This is bullshit. Ma, do you really think we belong here? These people have their own way of living and we don't fit."

"Problems will occur no matter where we go, so it's best you get tougher skin and roll with the punches," she said. While my mother was talking, I blocked her out. My eyes landed on the guy that I couldn't get out of my head. There he was just a few feet away wearing jean shorts, a wife beater and a pair of Jordans. His wild hair hung past his shoulders. Zambezi's presence made everything around me move in slow motion. He was with two other guys who looked to be around his age. I cringed when he wrapped his arms around Laguna and kissed her lips. While he was hugging her, our eyes locked.

"I'll be outside while you shop," I told my mother.

"Okay, give me five minutes," she said.

I rushed out of the market. When I got outside, I breathed a sigh of relief. The walls felt like they were closing in on me inside the fish market. I sat on the bench nearby to take in my surroundings. The small town was more than it let on. Something was hiding behind it and I had to figure it out because it probably wasn't safe for me and my mother. Someone sat next to me on the bench—it was Giva.

"Not having a good day?" she asked.

"I never have good days."

"We all have good days, chile. You're just stubborn and angry. Sometimes our feelings keep us from seeing our truth," she said.

"I see things all the time, but it doesn't mean it's real."

Giva laughed then went inside her knapsack. She pulled out a plastic bottle of water.

"You look thirsty," Giva said, handing me the water.

"No, thanks."

Giva seemed like a nice woman but I didn't trust the people in the town yet.

"I had a fish once. It was a beautiful fish. I couldn't wait to leave school just so I could go home and feed her. I named her Gold because she shined like a piece of jewelry. Anyway, Gold stopped swimming around in her bowl after a while. She'd just lay at the bottom. She was dying because she was taken out of her habitat. In order for her to survive, I had to put her back where I got her from. If you don't succumb to your natural habitat, you will die," Giva said.

"Are you telling me that I'll die if I don't get into the water? I take baths in water every day and nothing happens."

"Taking water out of a lake for a bath is the same as taking a fish out of its habitat. It's not the same, Shore. Your spirit is very special. It's a gift from our god. You were never supposed to live amongst humans for this long," Giva said.

"Are you ready, Shore?" my mother called out. When I turned back around, Giva was gone. I only turned my head for a split second and she just disappeared.

*I need to leave! I'm scared of this town. If I'm dying, wouldn't I be dead already? Giva must be some kind of witch. I told mother they exist. It could've been her all along, talking to me from the lake. That's it, I'm staying away from Giva.*

"Yes, I been ready!" I called out.

I got off the bench and grabbed a basket from my mother.

*I never thought I'd be saying this, but I can't wait to get to the cabin!*

# Zambezi

"Who are you looking for?" Laguna asked after we left the market.

I don't know why I cared about Shore seeing me hugged up on Laguna. Maybe it was the look in her eyes when she saw me. She expected something from me, but what? She didn't have to say it because her body spoke for her. Shore was a complete stranger; it had only been a day since we met but I couldn't get her face out of my head. I've seen a lot of women in my life, but Shore's beauty was enough to make all the women in the town envy her.

"Nobody," I finally answered after I noticed Shore was gone. My baby brother walked out the market along with Laguna's sister, Ara.

"So, what time are y'all picking us up? I hope we go to a better club tonight. The last one we went to was full of loud and raunchy people," Ara said. Ara and Laguna were almost identical, but Ara was shorter and a shade darker. They both had stuck-up attitudes and were clingy. I was getting bored with Laguna already and we'd only been messing around for two months. My brother, Bay, was practically stuck up Ara's ass.

"I'm chilling tonight but y'all can have fun," I said.

"Come on, bro. We've been talking about this for a few days. This town gives me a headache," Bay replied.

"I'm not a teenager anymore. That club shit is getting lame. Besides, I gotta go fishing for father tomorrow."

"Didn't the new girl move into the cabin by the lake? It's all making sense now. Was she who you were looking for? Stay away from her, Zambezi, and I mean it. I'll kill the whore if I have to," Laguna said.

"Yeah, I go fishing where Shore lives and I'm not gonna stop. I'll holla at you later."

Laguna followed me down the sidewalk, fussing and complaining about me not doing what she wanted me to do.

"So many men here want me but here I am wasting my time with you," Laguna said.

"Go entertain them then because I don't give a fuck. I'm not going to get jealous over you, so we can end this right now."

*Damn, that was easy!*

"Are you breaking up with me?"

"Listen, this isn't getting anywhere. My patience isn't set up for this situation."

"SITUATION?" Laguna screamed.

"Go home!"

Laguna walked away. It was the first time I got inside her head, so she could obey me. Hopefully, she wouldn't remember our argument. I was able to manipulate the mind, but it was considered a sin within my family. My parents would shit a brick if they knew I'd done it twice in the past few days. My mother called my abilities wicked and used to beat me for them when I was younger. She also refers to me as a sea devil, but I had a feeling the gold necklace I wore was the reason behind my ability.

**An hour later...**

My mother was sitting on the front porch when I arrived home. She was burning her special candles which were made out of fish oil and many other minerals from the water. The smell was unpleasant and reminded me of burnt fish blood. When she saw me coming, she blew out her candles. I sat next to her on the porch and there was a silence between us. Adwoa wasn't my real mother. I was two years old when she met my father. My birth mother disappeared after she had me. Although Adwoa raised me, we didn't have a strong bond the same as she had with my brother, Bay.

"Your father is in the back of the house in case you're looking for him," she said without looking at me.

"I wanted to talk to you about something."

Adwoa looked at me, her eyes turning to an emerald green, as gray scales covered her hands. She was getting agitated already. After the scales disappeared and her eyes turned back to dark brown, she stood up from her chair.

"Stay away from that girl, Shore. She's trouble to you and the rest of this town," Adwoa said.

"That's funny, Laguna told me the same thing. I want to know why Shore is here. She smells like a human, but something lingers around her. What is she?"

"She's trouble and that's all you need to know," Adwoa said.

"No disrespect, but y'all can't tell me what to do. I'll figure it out myself. Humans from the outside don't just show up here, Adwoa. Plus, Shore's cabin is right by the lake where the water fairies swim."

"If you go near that girl, I will have you banned from this town. You will not bring shame to this family. Set an example for your little brother and don't let temptation lure you in because once it does, you won't be able to come from that. I'll be expecting you to be at dinner tonight," she said. Adwoa went into the cabin with the screen door slamming behind her. Instead of going into the house, I went next door to my cabin. I'd had my own place since I was fifteen. Adwoa was too strict so I had to get my own space. I built the cabin myself. Every weekend, I went into the inner-city for library books on building houses. Adwoa whooped me because she thought I was acting "too human." Adwoa hated humans and because of it, she rarely spoke to anyone.

I almost tripped over Laguna's heels when I walked into my cabin. She purposely left them in the middle of the floor in case I brought another woman to my home. My father walked into my cabin with muddy boots, leaving a trail behind him. He grabbed a bottle of Hennessey off the counter in the kitchen and drank half of it in one gulp.

"Adwoa told me you backtalked her. You know I don't tolerate that kind of behavior. She's done a lot for you, maybe you should appreciate her."

My father was the owner of the big market in town; me and a few others in town helped him build it. His life circled around Adwoa, Bay and his market. Me, on the other hand, felt more like a baby brother to him opposed to his first born.

"I'm not fuckin' Adwoa, you are. I don't have to listen to her bullshit because you let her control this family. Sorry, Father. I'm not a boy anymore and I damn sure am not going to keep hearing about Adwoa's psychotic ass."

He slammed his fist into the counter, splitting it in half.

"Don't make me kill you, Zambezi! Adwoa said you want to know more about that girl who lives by the lake. She knows something about them and if she says stay away from her then that's what you should do!" He pointed a finger at me.

"Now I'm really curious about her."

"Talk to me, son. It's just you and me. Tell me what is wrong with you. Do you hate your family?" he asked in a calmer tone. I grabbed the bottle of liquor off the kitchen's island and poured some into a glass.

"Do you know why I go to the lake to catch fish for you? I've been catching fish for you since I was five years old, Father. That's the only time you look at me as your son. 'til this day, I'm still looking for the same shit from you, and what do you do? Storm into my home to talk about what

Adwoa wants. How about asking me how my day went the same as you do with Bay?"

"Bay is not a man yet, but you are," he said.

"You're right, Father. I am a man, therefore you and Adwoa can't tell me what to do. I'm ready to take a shower then go into the city. Maybe I'll bring a human woman back, so we can make noises all night long. Hopefully your precious piranha doesn't get too pissed off."

My father walked out the cabin, leaving the door wide-open. He hated when I called Adwoa a piranha. Matter of fact, he didn't care about anything I had to say unless it was an insult towards Adwoa. I shrugged it off then headed upstairs to take a shower.

**\*\*\*\*\*\*\*\*\*\***

**Three hours later...**

"The old man would bite your head off if he knew you had a car," my friend, Cascade said. He was riding in the passenger seat smoking kush wrapped up in seaweed. I had a car that I kept parked outside of our town. My family didn't know about my second life. I owned two fish markets in the inner-city where I sold the best seafood. Most of the customers owned five-star restaurants. The only reason I stayed in Oland was because of my brother, Bay. Oland was located in Virginia, three hours away from D.C. So, whenever I wanted to experience the night life, I had a long drive, but it was worth getting out of the small and boring town.

"Yo, don't burn a hole in my seat! I just got this," I said, and he chuckled. Cascade had Indian roots and he was also human. The Native Americans in our town, Oland, also worshipped the water people but they didn't know they existed. They heard stories of them through the elders who claimed they had seen them while fishing. To most, water people were myths. The Indians who had offspring by the water people didn't know their offspring were immortals. Once their off spring were old enough, they'd leave home and never return. As long as the humans didn't know of our real existence, they weren't a threat. Other than the differences, everyone lived as if it was the old times.

"Who told you to roll up kush in seaweed anyway?"

"Your brother. No lie, bro, this shit have me high for two days," Cascade said.

"Bay is gonna turn you into a fiend," I chuckled.

I pulled up to a valet line in front of a club in D.C. While I was waiting for the valet driver to come to my car, I was scoping out the human women who were waiting in line.

"This is why I hate Oland. Nothing but bougie, arrogant and devious women live back home," Cascade said.

"Laguna and her gang."

"Speaking of which, they said you broke up with her," he replied.

"I had to. Besides, the single life is my way of life. I'll never settle down, bro. Might as well enjoy sleeping with varieties of women while we're young."

The valet dude opened the door and I got out of the driver's seat, so he could park. Cascade was still in the passenger's seat smoking.

"Get out, muthafucka!"

"Oh damn. Aye, bro. You wanna hit this?" Cascade asked the valet dude.

"Naw, I'll lose my job. What kind of roll up is that?" he replied.

"Seaweed," Cascade replied.

"Oh word? I gotta try it," he said as Cascade was getting out the car.


Instead of waiting in line, I went to the door. The owner of the club shopped at my market. All I had to do was give them my name and they gave me my own private section.

"What's up, Zam? You don't have any sexy lil' shorties with you tonight?" the bouncer at the door asked.

"Naw, just a chill night, you feel me?"

"Yeah, man, no doubt. I'm ready to text Trina so she can have your section ready by the time you make it upstairs," he said.

"Okay, bet."

The bouncer moved the rope so me and Cascade could enter the club. The rap music was loud and the smell of weed, sweat and perfume filled the air.

"Damn, she phat," Cascade said when three girls passed us. The one in the short black dress caught my eye. She was curvy with a set of thick meaty legs. Her ass wasn't that plump, but she made up for it with the rack she had on her chest. We went upstairs where the VIP sections and the strippers were. Trina was sitting two buckets of champagne and Hennessey on the table when I approached the section.

"Let me know if you need anything else," Trina told me. She eyed Cascade and he pretended not to see her. Trina was feeling him. She grabbed one of his cornrows and twirled it around her finger. Trina wasn't attractive, but she was cool. Hanging around her sometimes was like being around a homeboy.

"When are you gonna come back to my place?" Trina asked Cascade.

"You know I got a girl, right?" Cascade lied.

"She can come, too," Trina said before walking off.

"Bro, when you gonna bring your talent to the inner-city?" I asked Cascade.

Cascade could practically make anything: paint, spices, tea, coffee and a lot of other things. His family worked inside my father's market. All the ingredients they used came from the earth.

"My parents be tripping. I can't be as free as you. They'll shit a brick if they knew I came to the city to party with you. They believe these places have evil spirits and it'll poison my soul. It's stressful," he said.

"Tell me about it. Soon, I'm going to live out here. Oland has nothing to offer me anymore."

"I'll join you after I stock up my supplies," he said.

The girl with the short black dress and her friends sat in a section across from ours. She was wearing a Happy Birthday tiara. She waved at me and I gave her a head nod.

"Have you met the new girl in town yet? I heard she's a dime," Cascade said, breaking me out of my thoughts. I was trying to get inside black dress head, to know her name, her age and what kind of drink she liked.

"Yeah, I met Shore. She's from the city."

"Oh word? An inner-city chick in Oland? You gotta tell me where she lives so I can bring her a gift," he said. Maybe it was the liquor I was drinking or the contact I caught from Cascade smoking in my car, but Shore was off limits.

*What in the fuck am I thinking about? Naw, she isn't mine. I barely know her. But damn if she isn't beautiful and smells like coconut milk.*

"Let's get off that subject, bro. I don't even wanna think about Oland right now or the people in it," I replied.

A woman came over to our section. She was with the birthday girl, the one Cascade was interested in.

"My friend wants to know why you keep looking at her. Why don't y'all come over?" she said to me.

"What's your name?" Cascade asked.

"Shalonda. What's yours?"

"Cascade."

"Like the dish washer soap?" she asked.

"Naw, like the waterfalls," he replied.

"Why your friend didn't come over here?" I asked her.

"She's shy," Shalonda lied.

Her friend wasn't shy, she wanted me to bite the bait. Shy women couldn't bear lustful stares. Most of the time, they'd look away and pretend it didn't happen, sorta like Shore.

"That girl ain't shy. Tell her to come over and sit on my lap," I replied.

Shalonda waved her friend over and she came. Their other friend followed her. They were all in our section. Black dress tried to sit down next to me, but I pulled her onto my lap.

"What's your name?"

"Natasha but my friends call me Nae-Nae. What's yours?" she asked while staring at my lips. Natasha wanted me to fuck her. I could feel her heat and smell the arousal coming between her legs.

"Zambezi."

"Like the Zambezi river? I like that," she said.

"What do you have planned for tonight?"

"Nothing, but I don't want to stop celebrating. So, we're having something at my hotel room in Fort Washington. Maybe you and your friend can join us," she said.

"Yeah, we can slide through."

Cascade rolled up a blunt for the ladies. Natasha was giving me a lap dance without wearing anything underneath her dress. My dick was pressed against my jeans, aching to be released. Her pussy was warm and wet. Although I only wanted one thing from her, I respected her. I didn't grope her or feel on her sexually. My desires carried to the bedroom.

## Four hours later...

Cascade and two of Natasha's friends were in the living room of Natasha's hotel room. I was on the bed, waiting for Natasha to come out the shower. It was four o'clock in the morning and I wanted to be home before sunrise. Seconds later, she walked out the bathroom with a towel wrapped around her. The steam from the shower followed her, causing the scent of her soap to linger. She smelled like mint and strawberries. I sat up and she straddled me, her towel dropping to the floor. Her perky breasts were against my lips while I cupped her ass. A moan slipped from her mouth when I placed her nipple between my lips. She reached underneath her to free my dick from my pants. My girth intimidated her.

"I'll be gentle."

Moments later, Natasha was bent over the bed, receiving every inch of my shaft. The bed beneath us was soaking wet from her squirting. Her loud moans filled the room along with the sounds of her pussy gushing down her legs.

"FUCCCCCKKKKKKKK!" she screamed while I pounded into her canal. I stretched her, probably ruining her for the next man's pleasure. Natasha pulled the sheets off the bed and stuffed them inside her mouth when I went deeper.

"It's in my stomach! It's in my stomach!" she cried out, but I was finished. When I pulled out of her, she fell onto the bed with her body covered in sweat. I went inside the bathroom to release my sperm inside the toilet. Natasha limped into the bathroom and asked me to shower with her.

*I'll scare the shit out of you.*

"I gotta get up early to do something for my pops. Can I call you later?"

She wrapped her arms around me and kissed my abdomen. Natasha was more than a foot shorter than me.

"I want you to stay," she said.

*Here we go again.*

"Aight, but I gotta leave in a few hours."

"That's all I need," she said while getting on her knees.

She took me into her mouth, wanting to go another round.

*I'm gonna put her to sleep then sneak out. Yeah, that's what I'm gonna do.*

An hour later, I was fully dressed and ready to leave. Cascade was sleeping on the floor between Natasha's two naked friends.

"Wake up, bro! I'm ready to go."

He quietly slid from between them and I turned my head, so he could get dressed. One of the girls started to move, so Cascade grabbed his shoes and we rushed out the door.

"That was wild, bro. My first time having a three-some," he said, putting his shoes on in the hallway.

The sun was out when we walked out of the hotel. Cascade cursed to himself because he had to hurry home to help his parents set up the stand at the market. Once we got into the car, I drove off, speeding to a place I hated the most—Oland.

# Shore

## A week later...

My mother came into my room with a cup of herbal soup. She got it from the market in town. When she mentioned Giva made it, I refused to eat it. My body was weak, and it felt like sharp shards of glass were cutting at my throat when I breathed. The seizures were getting worse.

"I have to take you to the emergency room," my mother said.

"The car won't make it and we don't have a phone to call 9-1-1. It'll pass by soon," I assured her.

"Eat the soup," she said.

"I don't want nothing from Giva. Those peaches from her stand made me sick. She's trying to kill me."

"I would've gotten sick, too, Shore. I ate everything you ate from Giva. Stop thinking she's trying to kill you!"

My mother left out of my room to get me a glass of water. A sharp pain rippled through my abdomen, taking my breath away. The room changed again for the tenth time. The furniture was old, and there was a shadow in the corner of my room. I couldn't speak or move. Whenever it came, everything was silent. It was hot and muggy inside the cabin, but I was freezing. The shadow came closer. It was in the form of a human, but the body was made of water. I could tell by the shape of the shadow it was a woman.

*Ma! Where are you? Please come quick!*

My eyes wouldn't blink as I tried to force them to move. I was screaming inside of my head, hoping it heard me. *GET AWAY FROM ME!*

When my mother came into the room, the shadow disappeared down my throat. It was drowning me. My mother dropped the glass of water on the floor as she rushed over to my bed.

"Breathe, baby, breathe!" my mother cried while pressing down on my chest. A gurgling sound came from my throat and water poured from my eyes and nose. I was gasping for air. When she pulled me up, I threw up enough water for a bath.

"I don't know what's happening to you. You need to see Giva. I'm gonna go find her. She's an herb doctor and maybe she has a remedy to make you better," my mother said. I was too weak to respond. All I could do was nod my head. Hell, I was dying anyway. *What more could Giva do to me?* I asked myself.

The front door closed behind my mother after she left the cabin.

"Come out! I know you want to since she's gone! I know all about evil spirits. You want me to die so you can use my body? Well, I hope like hell you have these seizures, too, if you do. What do you want from me, huh? Is this your cabin? If so, we'll leave but please leave my mother out of this. She's a good woman and doesn't deserve it!" I said aloud. I waited for the spirit to come back but it didn't.

*Maybe it was just a seizure. Hell no, what am I thinking? I wouldn't be able to remember every detail if it was a seizure. Maybe the thing is coming back for me.*

While staring at the ceiling, I thought back to when I was six years old. My mother's job at the time was having a picnic by the beach. Something happened to me that day and I have been afraid of large bodies of water ever since...

## Fourteen years ago, ...

*An old-school song played out of the speakers next to the DJ's booth. I didn't know the words, but I bobbed my head to the beat. It was the music my mother listened to every Sunday while she cleaned our apartment. The beach was crowded. Some people were playing Frisbees, volley ball and a few kids were building sand castles. My mother was talking to her co-workers while I sat at the picnic table to eat a hot dog and chips.*

"Hey, you wanna play with us?" a white girl my age asked.

"My mother said I have to stay where she can see me."

"We're just going over there," she pointed.

Where the kids were playing wasn't too far from my mother. I figured she could see me, so I left the picnic table to follow the girl. There were five other kids next to the sand castles.

"Why do you have that helmet on your head?" a little boy asked.

"So, I won't hit my head when I fall."

"I like it. The Sailor Moon sticker is cool. I have one on my wall at home," the white girl said.

"My name is Shore," I told them. I was actually excited to play with them because kids in my neighborhood didn't like to play with me.

"My name is Rain," a brown-skinned girl replied. Her sea shell bracelet chimed as she moved her hand and I wanted one.

"This is boring," a little boy said.

"Maybe we should play tag in the water. We just can't go far out," the white girl said. She never told me her name, but it didn't matter because I was having fun making a castle with Rain.

"Where do you live?" I asked Rain.

"My mother told me I cannot tell anyone where we live," Rain replied.

"What school do you go?" I asked.

"I go to school where I live," she replied.

"I wanna go to school with you."

"My mother said only special people can go to my school. Do you wanna collect sea shells with me?" Rain asked.

"Okay!"

While the other kids were playing tag, me and Rain were at the end of the beach collecting seashells and pretty rocks. It seemed as if we were gone for a long time because the sun was going down and the music was no longer playing.

"Let's go swimming so we can catch bigger seashells," Rain said.

"I don't know how to swim."

"I'll hold your hand. The water isn't too deep," she said.

I shrugged my shoulders and followed Rain into the water. She was my only friend and I couldn't upset her. I didn't want her to think I wasn't normal like the other kids.

"It's cold," I giggled.

"Really? It feels good to me. Well, my mother said humans aren't like us," Rain laughed.

"SHORE! GET OUT OF THE WATER! A STORM IS COMING!" my mother yelled.

I turned around to warn Rain about the storm, but she was gone. I called out for her, but she didn't answer me.

"RAIN!" I shouted.

A bolt of lightning soared through the sky as the wind grew strong. People on the beach were yelling and screaming out to me. That's when I realized I was the only one in the water. My mother and a lifeguard were swimming out towards me. I was so into playing with Rain, I didn't realize how far out we were in the water. The waves were getting stronger, pulling my small body further away from my mother. I kicked and screamed but my limbs were failing. Suddenly, something underneath pulled me down into the water. A shiny woman with glowing scales swam around me. Her face was of a human and she had glowing eyes. She didn't have legs, she had the tail of a fish. She moved my hair out of my face, her sharp black nails puncturing my skin by accident. My mother read me a book called, The Mermaid, but in the book the mermaid was human from the waist up. The creature that swam around me had scales all over her body. She grabbed my hand and pulled me towards the beach. The fish woman disappeared to the bottom of the water after she led me to my mother.

"CALL 9-1-1!" the lifeguard called out when he pulled me out. Everyone was surrounding me while my mother cradled me.

*"She was underneath the waves for a long time. We have to see if she has water in her lungs," the lifeguard told my mother. A few hours later, a search team was looking for Rain, but she was missing...*

That day I lost a friend. My mother's co-workers didn't understand how a six-year-old who never swam before was able to survive those waves. When I went to the hospital, there wasn't any water in my lungs. I'll never forget the look on the doctor's face after I told him I was breathing underneath the water. But of course, they blamed the seizures for seeing the fish woman. My mother lost her job after that incident because her co-workers thought she was unfit, and it wasn't a good look for them especially since I was a child with a disability. After thinking about the beach, I mustered up the little bit of strength I had to get out of bed. My naked body was drenched in sweat and my head was pounding as I stumbled outside the cabin. I fell onto the grass because my legs were stiff. It was the lake that was causing me to get sick. Maybe the fish woman who saved me at the beach years ago was in the lake. A pair of hands helped me off the ground. My mother and Giva returned. My vision was blurry, and my stomach was nauseous.

"I don't know what to do!" my mother said while holding me up.

"She's dying, Sabrina. I don't think my herbs can help her," Giva said.

"Nooooooo. She was just fine a week ago," my mother said.

They helped me into the cabin and laid me on the rug in the kitchen area. Giva wet a rag and placed it over my forehead.

"Go to my wagon and bring me my bag," Giva told my mother and she stormed out of the house.

"I'm sooo cold," I whispered.

"Why are you so hardheaded, chile? Stop making up enemies in your head and listen to your elders. Nobody is trying to hurt you. I can heal you, but I need your mother away from the cabin. She's not a believer anymore," Giva said.

"I'm a mermaid? The visions, breathing under water and the need for the lake is a part of it? Please tell me I'm just sick and that this is all fake.

There is no such thing as a human fish. Tell me I'm crazy!"

"I don't know what a mermaid is, Shore. But I do know water spirits are real and they live inside us. We're people from the water. Your immortal spirit needs healing," Giva said.

"Let me die. I'm scared to be one. Being a human is all I know."

"Sorry, dear, but I can't do that," she said. Giva helped me off the floor and into my bedroom. She wrapped a sheet around my body. My mother came into the room with Giva's medicine bag. Giva opened her bag looking for the right remedies to soothe the pain in my stomach.

"Damn it. It's not here. You will have to go to the market. I'll write down what you need. I'll stay here with Shore to keep an eye on her," Giva told my mother. My mother looked at me with tear-filled eyes. She didn't want to leave me, but I assured her I was going to be okay. My mother went into her purse to get a pen and pad for Giva's list. After she wrote down the items, she kissed my forehead.

"Please take care of my daughter while I'm gone. She's all I have left."

"I'll treat her like she is mine. Now hurry before the market closes," Giva replied. My mother kissed me again before she stormed out the cabin. Giva grabbed a green stick from her bag and burned it.

"What is that?"

"Seaweed. It's going to ease the stomach pain for a little while. Inhale as much as you can," Giva said. A few deep inhales later, the pain was gone. My body didn't seem as stiff as it did before.

"What does it feel like to be inhuman? What will I do? You have to tell me something because death sounds better."

"What are you afraid of? The water is more of your home than living on land. The fish woman you saw years ago wasn't trying to hurt you. She saved you because she knew you wasn't ready to see your truth. Those waves at the beach were meant to carry you home," she said.

"How do you know?"

"I know everything," she said.

"What happened to Rain?"

"She lured you away from the humans. Rain is alive," Giva replied. I was relieved to hear about my friend.

"Where is she?"

"She's around," Giva replied.

There was a knock at the door and Giva went to answer it. I pulled the sheet up to my chin to hide my breasts. When I heard Zambezi's voice, I wanted to hide. I didn't have to look in a mirror to know I looked a hot ass mess.

"I told Shore I'll knock before fishing at the lake. Is she here?" he asked Giva.

"Yes, but she isn't feeling well. You can come in," Giva invited him. Maybe Giva didn't understand what embarrassment is because she wouldn't have let Zambezi into our cabin. When he walked into my bedroom, my center began throbbing and my nipples poked through the fabric of the sheet.

*I'm not supposed to be aroused while dying!*

"You came just in time. I need your help. We have to get her into the lake before her mother returns," Giva told Zambezi. Zambezi kneeled in front of me yet his tall frame still towered over mine while sitting on the bed.

"She's scared," he said over his shoulder to Giva.

"She'll be fine," Giva said nonchalantly, and I rolled my eyes.

"I can't swim."

Zambezi chuckled and Giva covered her mouth to mute her giggles.

"My fish died the other day from drowning, too," Zambezi said with a smirk.

*Cocky asshole!*

"I'll make you apologize for that later. Okay, come on, chump. Let's get this over with so I can fish," Zambezi said. He stood up and I clutched the sheet tighter to my body as I got up. I prayed the sheet hid my private areas. As soon as I took a step, my legs turned to noodles. Zambezi caught me in his arms and the scent from his hair almost made me moan. Here I was practically on my last leg and lusting after Laguna's man. Just two weeks ago, I was living in a roach-infested apartment building and not having any contact with men other than perverted Lester. Now, I was living in a cabin next to a magical lake in a hidden town with immortals while imagining Zambezi lying on top of me while our bodies moved like the waves in the ocean.

The sun was beginning to set when we walked outside. Zambezi carried me towards the lake with Giva in tow.

"This is non-sense! Put me down! I feel better now!" I shouted when Zambezi stepped into the lake. For a split second, Giva talked me into thinking everything that was happening was real. The fish swam towards Zambezi and it creeped me out again. Some of the fish were bigger than the rest. There was so many of them.

"Noooooo. It's a shark!"

"Does she always act like this?" Zambezi asked Giva and she shrugged her shoulders.

"She's just going through a lot right now," Giva replied.

"Chill the fuck out, Shore! Sharks aren't in this lake," Zambezi aggressively stated. I was getting on his nerves—honestly, I was getting on my own nerves. The town was draining me dry in just a short period of time. All I had to do was leave.

"I just want to wake up. This isn't real. Tell me why the water is important."

Zambezi looked at Giva, waiting for her approval. They wanted me to get in the water, but I couldn't for the life of me understand why I couldn't just drink it.

"Why is it a secret?" I asked again.

"You've become somewhat human after living on land for so long. The bottom of the lake will rebirth your spirit—your immortal spirit. We call this Lake Deep. If you die now, it'll be too late to revive you. Your true identity lies beneath," Giva said.

Zambezi lowered me into the water, but I couldn't let him go. My nails scratched at his arms as he pulled away from me.

"Noooooo! Don't let me go! I'm afraid. Please, don't!" I cried.

"She's not ready, Giva. She can't go like this. She has to be at peace with what she's doing!" Zambezi said.

"She's dying! Let her go so they can take her!" Giva yelled at Zambezi. The clouds above the lake were pitch-black and the waves were coming. They were the same waves that tried to take me at the beach. The water pulled me, and Zambezi's arm changed. Blueish green and gold skin soon covered his arms.

"Let her go!" Giva said.

"I can't, Giva, I can't. Let's just talk about this in the cabin. She isn't ready!" he yelled at her.

Zambezi pulled me away from the waves and the impact of them were stronger. Water from the lake washed up on the land and against the cabin. My body slipped underneath, and Zambezi pulled me towards him. My vision was clear as if I had on goggles. Something about Zambezi's body began feeling different. When I looked up, dark green glowing eyes were looking at me. Zambezi's body was slightly bigger than his usual frame. His chest and arms were more structured, defining each outline of his muscles. He was scary and beautifully unique at the same time. The necklace around his neck was embedded into his skin; it was a part of him. He wasn't a merman, he was a water creature. His canines reminded me of vampire teeth. Zambezi's hair turned into long dreadlocks with gold glowing tips. If you looked too fast, his body camouflaged with the background of the lake underneath. The fins on his arms and legs were solid and covered in a metallic gold shield. They were sharp enough to slice a human in half.  He swam circles around me to protect me from the fish women. There were around a dozen of them. The way Zambezi glided through the water reminded me of a shark—his kind were predators. While moving smoothly through the water, his long locs trailed behind him.

*Swim away, Shore. I can hold them off,* I heard Zambezi's thoughts.

Zambezi lowered me into the water, but I couldn't let him go. My nails scratched at his arms as he pulled away from me.

"Noooooo! Don't let me go! I'm afraid. Please, don't!" I cried.

"She's not ready, Giva. She can't go like this. She has to be at peace with what she's doing!" Zambezi said.

"She's dying! Let her go so they can take her!" Giva yelled at Zambezi. The clouds above the lake were pitch-black and the waves were coming. They were the same waves that tried to take me at the beach. The water pulled me, and Zambezi's arm changed. Blueish green and gold skin soon covered his arms.

"Let her go!" Giva said.

"I can't, Giva, I can't. Let's just talk about this in the cabin. She isn't ready!" he yelled at her.

Zambezi pulled me away from the waves and the impact of them were stronger. Water from the lake washed up on the land and against the cabin. My body slipped underneath, and Zambezi pulled me towards him. My vision was clear as if I had on goggles. Something about Zambezi's body began feeling different. When I looked up, dark green glowing eyes were looking at me. Zambezi's body was slightly bigger than his usual frame. His chest and arms were more structured, defining each outline of his muscles. He was scary and beautifully unique at the same time. The necklace around his neck was embedded into his skin; it was a part of him. He wasn't a merman, he was a water creature. His canines reminded me of vampire teeth. Zambezi's hair turned into long dreadlocks with gold glowing tips. If you looked too fast, his body camouflaged with the background of the lake underneath. The fins on his arms and legs were solid and covered in a metallic gold shield. They were sharp enough to slice a human in half. He swam circles around me to protect me from the fish women. There were around a dozen of them. The way Zambezi glided through the water reminded me of a shark—his kind were predators. While moving smoothly through the water, his long locs trailed behind him.

*Swim away, Shore. I can hold them off,* I heard Zambezi's thoughts.

I didn't want to leave him, but I had a chance to get away. Suddenly, a force knocked me over, crippling me; its force was too strong to escape, pushing me farther away from the land. As Zambezi made his way towards me. I reached out my hand to him, but the force snatched me away from him. More fish women surrounded him, there were around thirty of them. They weren't trying to kill him, they were using themselves as a wall to surround him. The only way to get through was to hurt them, but he didn't. A water spirit pulled me further down into the lake, where the water wasn't as clear. I stopped fighting, it was useless. At the very bottom of the lake was a leaf-shaped, large green glowing rock. A silhouette appeared in front of me seconds later. It was an outline of a woman. Something strange began happening; fish scales covered the silhouette, filling her in, almost like coloring a picture. It was the fish woman who saved me at the beach.

*It's you again. What do you want from me?*

She moved the hair out of my face, the same as she did when I was a little girl.

*You will understand soon,* she replied.

A burning sensation traveled through my veins, making them glow. The fish woman swam around, singing a beautiful melody. They weren't words, but it was soothing. She had me hypnotized as my body laid across the rock. Whatever she was doing to my spirit was painless. Matter of fact, I wanted to stay there and rest. All I could imagine was being in a spa with those soothing songs playing in the background. All of a sudden, dozens of fish women surrounded the rock. The feeling of serenity came to a halt when I felt myself drowning. I was no longer able to breathe under water. Water filled my lungs, suffocating me.

*Your spirit will no longer make you sick,* the water spirit said.

Before I closed my eyes, I caught a glimpse of Zambezi—he was too late.

# Zambezi

*I'm too late.*

The water spirits swam around Shore's body, healing her immortal soul. She was very sick, frail since the last time I saw her. Her skin had a blue complexion and her lips were dried out. I almost didn't recognize her when Giva invited me into the cabin. Even though they were saving her, I couldn't ignore her pleas for help. After the water spirit queen and her daughters were finished healing Shore, I rushed to her body, lifting her up from the rock. Jewel, the water goddess, swam to Shore's body and placed a necklace around her neck.

*Your kind isn't supposed to come down here. This rock is our territory,* Jewel said.

*My kind is what helped heal your waters, Jewel. I know you're very old, but your mind hasn't perished yet.*

*Be careful with your tongue unless you want your head to wash up on shore. This isn't any of your business now get out of my waters!*

Jewel's daughters surrounded me, and I held Shore's body close to mine.

*Leave him, he's no threat to us. His gift will humble him soon,* Jewel said to the others.

*What gift?* I asked.

*Take her to get some rest,* Jewel said, ignoring my question.

She and her daughters disappeared into the dark shadows of the water. Shore's eyes were fluttering, she was ready to wake up. I took her back above water. Giva rushed to Shore and pulled her out of the water. Shore's complexion was back to normal, but I noticed slight changes. She looked a few years younger and her hips were curvier. Her nipples were the shape of starfish and her hair was the color of aquamarine. Her nails were the same color as her hair. The necklace Jewel gave her was a locket.

"She's healed!" Giva clapped her hands. Giva's excitement faded away as she stared at me, she was looking at my side. I thought maybe I was injured but I wasn't, I had a marking on me instead. Giva turned Shore over on her side; Shore had the same symbol as me, embedded into her skin.

"Did you go near the rock? While it was healing her?" Giva asked.

"Yeah, what's the big deal?"

"Looks like the rock showed you your truth too. But since you're connected to Shore, you must protect her, or else someone close to you will die," Giva said.

"Jewel cursed me? That's why she let me go so freely. That ancient muthafucka."

"Speak of my sister that way and I'll cut your tongue!" Giva said.

"Jewel isn't my queen, Giva. I don't worship or obey her beliefs."

"It doesn't matter. We're all a part of the water. We must respect each other's beliefs when someone we care about is caught in the middle. Anyways, my job is done. It's time for me to join my queen," Giva said. She pulled away from Shore and returned to the water. Her fish tail caused a gigantic wave when she dived under to join her clan. I picked up Shore and carried her to the cabin and back to her bed. She was flinching and mumbling something in a different language.

*"Tiya juti mi casti ju rue,"* she whispered.

The front door to the cabin opened. Shore's mother walked into the bedroom with a paper bag in her hand.

"Where is Giva?" she asked.

"She's gone. Shore is better now," I replied.

"You're Adwoa's son, right?" she asked. She sat next to Shore on the bed then kissed her forehead.

"Yeah."

"And you were fishing here? Shore said I pulled a gun out on you, but I can't seem to remember. I apologize wholeheartedly if I did. Sometimes I get a little carried away," she said. She examined Shore's locket, then tried to open it, but it wouldn't budge.

"What is this?"

"A welcoming gift," I replied.

"I've seen one of these before," she said in confusion.

I silently listened to Sabrina's thoughts as she talked. The memories she had weren't of water fairies. I only saw images of her and Shore.

"Mother," Shore whispered with her eyes closed.

"I'm here, baby. I'm here," Sabrina replied.

I wondered how Sabrina didn't know anything about the water fairies when she brought her immortal daughter to a lake with immortal beings.

"Zambeziiii. Umm, Zambezi."

Shore placed her hand between her legs and rubbed her pussy. She was dreaming about me. Having naughty thoughts of me on top, inside of her.

"What in the fuck did Giva give my child while I was gone?"

Sabrina left out of the room and came back with a glass bottle of milk. She told me to sit her daughter up while she poured milk down her throat.

"What's the milk for?"

"To sober her up. Have you seen a crackhead before? Giva gave my child drugs," Sabrina said. I took the milk from her because Shore wasn't high, she was recovering from her healing.

"She's just in a deep sleep. The herbs make her sleep well."

"My daughter is a virgin. She's not supposed to be doing this kind of shit," she said, pacing back and forth across the floor.

"Wait a damn minute!" she paused and looked at me.

"Have you been sticking your little shrimp in my daughter? See, I knew something was up when that big forehead child, Iguana, threatened my daughter," she said. I tried to keep a straight face, but a chuckle slipped out. Sabrina slapped me in the back of my head.

"Aight, chill out! I haven't touched your daughter in that way. This is my second time being around her. Laguna threatens everybody."

"My daughter isn't ready for that. I'm just warning you now. She has epilepsy and I don't need some no-good boy stressing her out, so you can leave and don't come back," Sabrina said.

"Tell her I'll see her around when she wakes up."

"Did you not just hear what I said?" Sabrina spat.

"Goodnight."

I left out of Shore's cabin and cut through the woods to head home. Adwoa was right about one thing. I needed to stay away from Shore. It wasn't her fault that I went on the water fairy's territory which was more of a reason I had to stay away— she was changing my life already.

My father's cabin was quiet when I got there. Thankfully, they were sleeping so I could sneak in the house without them seeing my marking. I headed straight to the kitchen when I walked into my house to grab a knife.

*This better work because I'm not ready for that commitment to Shore. In order to protect her, I'll have to spend my life with her. That's a bunch of bullshit!*

The knife pierced through my skin. Blood dripped on the floor and the pain was excruciating. My teeth pierced through my lip from gritting too hard. After I was finished cutting the symbol off my body, I fell onto my knees in a puddle of blood—I was very weak.

"Zambezi! You home?" my brother yelled out when he came into my cabin. I grabbed a hand towel and pressed it against my side.

"Don't come in here!" I yelled out.

"I need to talk to you about something," he said. He stepped in a puddle of my blood when he walked into the kitchen.

"What happened?" he rushed to me, but I pulled away.

"I thought I told you to knock before walking into my shit?" I gritted.

"I was knocking but you didn't answer. I smelled blood, so I came in. Who did this?" Bay asked with a vein popping out of his neck; he was ready to turn.

"Long story, little brother. Let's just say, water fairies are wicked."

He helped me off the floor and all of a sudden, the pain was gone. I removed the hand towel from my wound and it was gone. My wound was healed and the symbol was back.

"FUCK!" I yelled out and punched the wall.

"This can't be real. They're fucking with me. This can't be real!" I paced back and forth. Bay stared at me in confusion.

"You bitchin' about a tattoo?" he asked with a raised eyebrow.

"This is more than that, brother. I'm a water fairy's protector for life. Do you know what that means? I have to bring her everywhere with me. Even when I get some pussy."

"Who is it?" he asked.

"Shore."

"The girl our parents told you to stay away from? Damn, bro. You about to get a human ass whipping," he chuckled. I wanted to knock the shit out of him.

"Yeah, her. I wanted to rip Jewel's head off."

"Wait, you met Jewel? The water fairy, queen, Jewel? Is she sexy, bro?"

"Do you see why I can't tell you personal shit? I'm not into MILFS," I replied.

"What is that?"

"You never watched p— Neva mind. Don't tell anyone about this. If you do, I'm gonna pull all your skin back and feed you to the gators. I'm serious, brother. You better not say a fuckin' word," I said.

"I'm not a snitch, damn," he replied.

"What do you want to talk about? You said that's why you came here."

"I want in," he said.

"Want in on what?"

"Your business with the humans," he replied.

"How do you know about that?"

"You catch a lot of seafood but only half goes to father's market. The other half you put on your boat. Plus, I followed you yesterday until your boat reached the dock by your market. The Shore, huh? Looks like you met the girl you named your market after," he said.

"You swam for all those hours, to be in my business? You're just like your mother. So, what now? You're gonna blackmail me?"

"No, I want in. You think I like living here? Well, I don't. Adwoa treats me like I don't have hair on my testicles. Bro, I'll be twenty soon and still have a curfew. Mother is trying to weaken us the way she did Father. I don't want to be like him. He doesn't even live like the leader he used to be," Bay said.

"Their golden child wants to escape. How do you think they'll feel about that? Father would definitely try and rip out my soul if he knew I helped you."

"I don't care about that. I'll be ready when you are," he said, walking towards the door. I called out to him.

"Get Adwoa to braid your hair. You gotta look presentable at my place of business."

"Get some rest, bro," he said and closed the door behind him.

When Giva told me someone close to me would die if I failed Shore, I thought of Bay. I wouldn't dare tell him his life was on the line. All I had to do was protect Shore. But I wondered what I had to protect her from?

*What else is out there that can harm a water fairy?* I thought to myself.

# Shore

"**S**hore!"

My eyes fluttered when I heard my mother's voice. I was exhausted, my body felt like it ran a hundred miles. I was awake but dreaming. I've dreamt of the water fairy queen, the sea and Zambezi.

"Shore! Get up so you can eat!" she yelled.

My vision was blurry when I opened my eyes. I held my hands in front of me to make sure I didn't have any fins. My memory was vague of what happened at the bottom of Lake Deep. All I could remember was the feeling of drowning and Zambezi coming to save me. My mother pulled me up, so I could drink a glass of water. My throat was very sore. When I coughed, two small fish came up and got into my water glass.

"What in the hell is really going on, Shore? I was only gone for two hours yesterday and I come back with a boy half naked sitting in your bedroom watching you sleep. And my gosh, look at your hair, it's trashy. What made you get this color? Oh, and you have a tattoo," she fired off. I rushed out of bed and ran to the mirror.

"Oh, my heavens. I look like a BRATZ doll!" I screamed.

My hair was loud, my boobs were bigger than before. I looked closer into the mirror and my nipples were shaped like starfish. My skin was clearer and that odd pressure on my brain that gave me permanent headaches was gone. My nails were too long, way out of my comfort zone, especially since they were sharp and pointy. I was a short square-nail type of girl.

"I need a drink," my mother expressed.

She opened the window and was ready to toss the fish out inside the glass cup, but I took it from her. I grabbed a glass bowl off the kitchen table we used for flowers and rushed outside. My mother ran out behind me telling me to get back inside because I was naked. The fish needed water from the lake. After I filled up the glass bowl, I placed them inside.

"Really, Shore? You ran out of the house to save fish? How did they get in your throat anyway?" she asked.

"Giva used them to heal me," I lied.

"Giva must've used something else because you don't look like my daughter. And why do your nipples look like that? You look like you lost your damn mind," she said. I heard giggling, looked out into the lake and didn't see anyone.

*Shore is getting in trouble,* the voices echoed in my head. The lake was talking to me again and it wasn't anyone else but the water fairies.

*Mind your business, bitches! Oops, I'm so sorry. That slipped out.*

*That was a good one. We'll be back later,* they replied.

"SHORE! Do you hear me talking to you?" Sabrina asked.

"I don't know what you want me to say. What is wrong with my makeover?"

"You were beautiful the way you were. It's that tall curly-haired boy, huh? You didn't start acting strange until you met him," she said.

"I'm not sick anymore, Mother. Maybe you should let me make up the times where I couldn't do certain things. I feel so happy right now just by looking at the sun."

"You're right but a mother's job is never done. I'm going to always voice my concern," she said. I hugged my mother, picking her up off the ground and squeezed her.

"I can't breathe," she said.

I put her down, after realizing how strong I'd become.

"Come in the house and hurry up before someone sees you. Help me prepare breakfast. You need to eat something," she said while we headed towards the cabin.

"Ohh no you don't. Get those things off my table," Sabrina said when I placed the fish bowl on the kitchen table.

"What's wrong with them?"

"Do they look like normal fish to you? Their eyes are glowing, and I think they're staring at me. I don't do well with pets," she said.

"You need to rest, Mother. I'll fix breakfast. You've been waiting on me and not getting any rest."

"Okay, baby," she said.

She went into the closet-sized bedroom where she slept. The cabin was falling apart, and the floors were rotting out. I wasn't sick anymore, so I could get a job.

*Maybe we can move into a nicer cabin by the market if I start working.*

The water pail was empty. I had to go outside to get water out of the lake, so I could boil potatoes.

*We need an oven. I'm sick of boiling water before we use it to cook with.*

I got dressed in an oversized T-shirt and track shorts before grabbing the water pail and heading back out the cabin.

While kneeling down near the lake, a face with blue and gold scales appeared in the water and scared the shit out of me. I dropped the water pail as my heart was beating out of my chest. The thing was scared of me, too.

"Who are you?" I asked.

I waved my hand in front of my face and it mimicked me. That's when I realized I was the reflection. My eyes were more slanted than usual, and my hair was in a wild, unmanageable mane.

*This is cannot be real. Maybe I'm dead and stuck in a non-existent world. That's gotta be it.*

A hand touched my shoulder and I was ready to scream until someone covered my mouth while snatching me off the ground.

"I'm not trying to alert your mother so be quiet," the familiar voice said.

When I turned around, the butterflies I had in my stomach were uncontrollable. Zambezi was wearing a sleeveless shirt and his hair was in two cornrows. He smelled like the ocean breeze Febreze mixed with cocoa butter.

"Please don't do that again. My nerves are very bad now."

"My bad about that. I had to sneak up on you because your mother threatened me last night," he chuckled. His teeth were even perfect but if you stared too long, his canines were slightly longer and sharper than a human's.

"My mother thinks I'm a baby."

"I respect it though," he said. He put his hands in his pockets and I thought it was cute. Zambezi seemed to have been stalling about asking me something. He then rubbed the back of his neck.

"Okay, fuck it. We got matching tattoos—well, markings," he came out and said. He lifted up his shirt and there it was, the same marking I had on my left side.

"It must be some type of connection to the water."

"Naw, beautiful. It's wayyyy deeper than that. I wish it was that simple, but I belong to you. Not in that way, though, but I gotta protect you or else your squad is gonna fuck with me. With that being said, you gotta come to the inner-city with me. Please don't ask me shit, just get dressed and hurry up," he said with an attitude.

*He's mad because he has to protect me? Wow! Just when I thought I was like the Little Mermaid and he was gonna be my prince charming. Fuck those fairytales.*

"I'm not going anywhere. I have to make my mother breakfast," I said while walking away.

"She gotta fix her own breakfast!" he called out.

"Get off my property!" I said, running towards the cabin. Zambezi ran after me and snatched me up by the shirt, ripping it straight down the middle.

"Let's make something clear really quick. I do not chase women, not now, not ever! My brother's life is on the line and we will not fuck this up. If something happens to you, something happens to him. You can follow that trail through the woods or I'll carry you. Which one is it gonna be?"

Honestly, I didn't like it one bit. I was thinking Zambezi was going to hang out with me on his own, not because he had to. Not only did I have to go, he was in a position to control me. Just when I thought I had more freedom because I was healed, it was taken away.

"I don't go places with strangers."

"Now, I'm a stranger? You were aroused for me last night. Don't believe me, ask your mother. She already thinks we're fuckin'," he said.

*Maybe I should just die from embarrassment.*

"Okay, I can play your little game, but I won't be empty-handed. You have to pay me, so I can fix this house up," I replied.

"I can fix it myself but you gotta do what I say. Deal?" he asked.

"One more thing."

"Bruh, what the fuck!" He threw his hands up in frustration.

"I want that necklace."

Zambezi's vein protruded out of his neck as he clenched his fist. His eyes turned and the necklace around his neck sizzled into his skin—he wanted to turn on me. His energy wasn't a good one and almost frightened me, but I stood my ground. The simple things I asked for couldn't compare to the humiliation I had to deal with from him bossing me around.

"This is all I have left of my mother and you want to take it away?"

"Fine, buy me one like it and I'll be glued to your hip like a starfish," I spat.

"Good, now come on. My brother is waiting for me," he said.

"I can't go like this."

"Two minutes to change now hurry up," he said.

Zambezi's attitude towards me somewhat crushed me. The first time I met him, he was sweet to me then suddenly he hated me.


Sabrina was asleep when I went into the house. I changed into a pair of gray leggings, a jersey top with a pair of Nike slides. Before I left the cabin, I wrote my mother a note telling her I went to the market. Zambezi was waiting for me by the woods when I left the cabin.

"You could've waited until I took a bath."

"Where we're going doesn't require a bath. Besides, you smell good," he said, and I rolled my eyes. While I walked behind him, I smelled under my arms to make sure I didn't stink.

"How long is this walk?"

"We're almost there," he said.

We walked down a hill and there were animal bones sprawled out everywhere. I covered my nose after inhaling a pungent smell of an animal's carcass. A few feet away, turkey buzzards were eating a mangled deer. The area wasn't a beautiful scenery like Lake Deep. We were in a marsh. Ten minutes later, we approached a dock. A boy that resembled Zambezi was sitting on the boat smoking a blunt. He had a more youthful face, but he was very handsome nonetheless.

"About time, bro!" he said when we approached the boat.

Zambezi jumped onto the boat and I stood on the dock with my arms crossed.

*I'm so not in the mood for this bullshit!*

He held his hand out to me, "Come on," he said.

I grabbed his hand and he helped me onto the fishing boat.

"Didn't know your kind used boats."

"You think we should swim up into the city looking like three big-ass tropical fish?" Zambezi asked.

"Fuck him. How you are doing, beautiful?" his brother asked.

"I was good until your brother kidnapped me."

He passed me his blunt and I told him I didn't smoke.

"You gotta hit this one time," he said.

"Naw, Bay. She doesn't need it. Matter of fact, come up here with me, Shore," Zambezi called out while steering the boat.

"Naw, I'm good right here," I replied and took the blunt.

Zambezi stopped the boat to toss Bay's blunt out into the water.

"What you do that for? I just rolled that!" Bay yelled.

"I specifically told you that I didn't want you to walk around my place of business smelling like kush. You hard-headed, bro. Be respectful because I can turn this boat around and send you back home," Zambezi replied.

"Bossy-ass muthafucka," Bay mumbled.

Zambezi called me up to the front of the boat again.

*I wonder if he's jealous.*

"Sit right there where I can see you," he said when I went to the front.

His chocolate arms had small beads of sweat from being underneath the sun. The muscles in his upper body flexed while steering the boat away from the land. My thoughts were dirty and my clit throbbed hard enough to make my legs tremble.

"I think you might want to take care of that," Zambezi smirked, and I rolled my eyes.

"How about you stay out of my business."

"You having nasty thoughts about me is my business. Why are you a virgin anyway? Don't you come from a city?" he asked.

"I was always sick, so I didn't get out much."

Zambezi was quiet for the rest of the way. I wondered what he was thinking about and why I couldn't hear his thoughts the same way he heard mine. The ride took almost three hours. When we pulled up to a dock, there were five people waiting next to a small fish house called, The Shore.

"Nice name."

"Appreciate it, now I know someone with the name," he said.

"Zambezi is feeling you, too. I wouldn't trip over his behavior. He's always been that way and got a lot of beatings behind it, too," Bay interrupted. Zambezi tied his boat to the dock before he climbed off.

"You still salty about that blunt I threw out, huh?" Zambezi asked his brother.

"Saltier than a can of sardines," Bay said, and I giggled.

"Oh, so you laugh at his jokes but roll your eyes when I talk to you?" Zambezi asked me, giving me butterflies.

"You're an asshole, bro. I'm the ladies' man," Bay replied.

"Fool, shut up. I taught you how to talk to women," Zambezi said, helping me off the boat. He handled me like I was a small child. His strength and arrogance caused me to crave something I'd never had—dick.

*Get these dirty thoughts out of your head now!* I screamed inside my mind.


Bay and Zambezi were walking in front of me, and I couldn't make out what they were talking about. Bay was a few inches shorter than Zambezi but they both had the same athletic build, sorta like basketball players.

*Come swim with us, sister. The water is waiting for you.*

*Get out of my head,* I replied.

*Why don't you like us? We're your only friends. We come from the same reef, Shore, we're your family. Come and join us.*

I saw four water fairies swimming alongside of the dock while I was heading to the market. Their long fish-like tails sparkled underneath the water, they were beckoning me to come in.

*I'll tell you everything you want to know about yourself if you bring me a mirror. I need a new one,* the voice said.

*Fine!*

*It has to be big enough for our sisters to share. We're leaving now,* she replied.

I wanted them to come back, but I was off the dock and on the land where they couldn't see me anymore. Zambezi unlocked the back door to his market; we were in the storage area where he kept the seafood preserved. The clock on the wall read eleven o'clock.

"We open in thirty minutes," he said. He gave me and Bay work shirts with his logo on it along with rubber gloves.

"Once we leave here, we will go to my other location which is further down the river," Zambezi said.

"So, it's just us three?" I asked.

"Yeah, I usually do it by myself. Get ready cause the place is going to be crowded," he said. He handed me a roll of tickets to put in the ticket dispenser for the customers.

"What time will I get home? My mother is going to worry about me."

"You got a job now, Shore. Tell your mother you stepped into adulthood," Zambezi replied, grabbing large buckets of ice.

"I got some more kush in my pocket," Bay said to me when Zambezi left the freezer.

"Okay."

*This is gonna be a long day.*

## Three hours later...

Zambezi wasn't exaggerating when he said we were going to be busy. The market had over fifty people. He was handling the majority of the customers and even had conversations with a few.

"This is too much," I complained with sweat dripping down my face. Bay was grabbing jumbo male crabs and tossing them into a bucket from a cooler.

"Work at my father's market. It'll make you want to kill everyone!" Bay chuckled. I didn't know what to do. If it was up to me, I would've dumped all the seafood into the water to free them. I was never a fish eater; somehow, I was experiencing their pain.

"Excuse me. Can you tell me how much these shrimps run a dozen?" a black guy asked. He had a southern accent with shoulder-length locs. He was light-skinned and had a few tattoos on his arm. He was cute and had small freckles.

"Bay, how much for the gulf shrimp again?"

"Twenty-four a dozen if he wants the head on. Thirty-four if he wants the head off," Bay called out.

"I'll take two dozen with the head on," he replied.

I grabbed the shrimp and dumped them into a plastic bag along with ice. The stranger gave me cash and I placed it inside the register.

"I like that color on you. It highlights your face," he said about my hair.

"Thanks, I'm getting used to it."

"What's your name?" he asked.

"Shore," I replied.

"I'm Nerida. Do you live around here? My family just moved here a few weeks ago," he said.

"I don't live far."

"My father just opened up a seafood restaurant. It's called, Wild Caught. I'm a chef there and it's ocean view seating. Maybe you can come through. It's on the house," he said.

"I'll keep that in mind. Have a nice day," I smiled.

"You do the same, beautiful," he replied.

Zambezi was eyeing me when I turned around. I didn't see him come behind the counter.

"You know you can't go to that restaurant without me, right?" he asked. He was teasing me.

"Are you hating?"

"I'm just saying, I hope two can eat for free," he chuckled.

"I do not like you anymore."

"Good, it'll make my job easier. You have a customer," he said before walking off. I wanted to throw a butcher knife at the back of his neck. Bay waited until Zambezi was out of ear shot before he told me his brother was jealous.

"I was thinking the same thing, but I actually think your brother hates me," I replied. When I looked into Zambezi's direction, a woman was flirting with him and he was all smiles. My stomach cringed when she wrote her number down on a piece of paper.

*That bitch isn't all that!*


I went into the back to sit on a crate because the over-sized rubber boots on my feet were hurting. Working in a seafood market was hard work. Zambezi came into the back seconds later.

"Your feet hurt?" he asked.

"Very much."

He sat on the crate across from me and placed my feet in his lap. His hands easily took the pain away.

"This feels so good."

"Can't have you ruining your feet," he replied.

"How does Laguna feel about you flirting with different women and giving them foot massages?"

"I'm single," he said.

"I'm exhausted."

"We're ready to close soon. The other market isn't this busy and it's only by appointment. I just have three customers coming in," he replied.

"Doesn't sound like a regular fish market."

"That's because I don't sell regular seafood there," he replied.

"Don't tell me it's a water fairy."

Zambezi threw his back and roared in a deep laughter. I punched him in the chest and he laughed harder.

"Yo, you're funny as shit. But on the real, it's shark meat and things like that. Chefs with those two-hundred-dollar plates get their seafood from me," he replied. He traveled further up my leg, pressing his fingers into my inner-thighs while working his way back down to my foot. My essence spilled out of my slit, seeping through the thin material of my leggings. Zambezi saw it and I closed my legs, but he didn't stop massaging. Suddenly, my leggings ripped and the skin on my legs was stretching and pulling.

"Awww shit! Bay!" Zambezi yelled out. I fell over on the crate and my razor-sharp fins poked through my hips. Bay came into the back and froze when he saw me lying on the floor.

"Make it stop!" I screamed.

"Hold it down while I take Shore to the river," Zambezi told Bay. He picked me up and rushed me out the back door. My body was burning up and my throat ached from being dry—I needed water. Zambezi ran down the dock and jumped into the water with me in his arms. The water soothed my legs while they finished transforming. Half of my body was like a fish's and pearls decorated my hips. The fin on the end of my tail sparkled like glitter dust. My hair grew out, reaching the tip of my tail. At that moment, I was no longer in denial. Everything that was happening was real and my true identity was revealed.

"I think you got too aroused," Zambezi said.

I dived underneath, flapping my tail to splash him. He went underwater, his clothes shredding away from his body as he transformed. He grabbed my hand and pulled me further down towards the bottom. He swam on top of me, guiding me by my hips; he was teaching me how to swim.

*Use your back and your tail will follow.*

Zambezi let me go and I swam between two rocks. There was an old fishing boat at the bottom along with a human's skeleton.

*You'll see a lot of that. Sometimes they sink too deep and humans can't find them. Keep going,* he thought.

*Why can't I hear your thoughts on land?* I asked.

*Because it doesn't work like that.*


A group of catfish followed me and a wave of electricity from Zambezi's necklace killed them.

*What did you do that for?*

*I hate bottom feeders. Keep swimming and don't worry about me. You almost got it. You've been in the same spot for a while now.*

*I'm supposed to know this already if this is what I am.*

*Every being has to learn how to adapt to their habitat. Babies have to learn how to walk. Lions have to learn how to hunt and baby alligators have to figure out how to survive once they hatch,* he thought.

Zambezi grabbed me by the waist and pulled me up above water. After getting a closer look at him, Zambezi had skin of a reptile. I touched his face and a deep grunt came from his throat in a huffing sound.

"What are you?"

"A serpent," he replied, gazing at my lips.

"What is that?"

"A water dragon," he said. He went underneath the water and came back up. The clouds got darker, almost like the night. The trees blew, and the waves were picking up. A water blast came out of Zambezi's mouth and struck the clouds, making it thunderstorm then it stopped. The dark clouds uncovered the sun and the waves stopped.

"Show off."

Zambezi pulled me underneath and we swam back to the dock. Once we were close to land, he was human again, but I still had fins and a tail.

"I can't turn human."

"You have to. Concentrate," he said.

I went underneath the water, and Zambezi's bare dick was in my face.

*Oh wow, he's huge! No wonder he's some kind of dragon.*

He pulled me up again, but this time I was against his chest with his erection pressed against my stomach. Zambezi lowered himself into the water, so we could be face-to-face. My tail wrapped around him and he moved my hair away from my breasts. I couldn't form the words I wanted to speak because I was nervous. My tail was shrinking, and I could feel my toes all over again. Zambezi pulled away from me.

"See, you concentrated on that kiss you were waiting for. Now you're back to normal," he said. I felt played and humiliated once again. Instead of lashing out and speaking how I really felt, I took the curve he threw me like a champ.

"I don't have any clothes."

"I have some on the boat. They might be too big, but they'll do," he said. He pulled himself onto the boat and helped me up. I tried not to look at his naked backside, but I couldn't help it. His wet manhood slapped against his leg. I squeezed my thighs together and turned completely around to face the back of his market.

"Here you go," he said.

He handed me a T-shirt that was big enough to look like a dress on me. I thanked him for it and pulled it over my head.

"Don't think I don't notice your beauty. I'm not the only one who knows you're more than a diamond. It's hard to explain but I'm not the type of guy you want to fall for and you can see it, too. I'll be back. I'm going to help Bay close down the market," Zambezi said.

"Okay."

I waited until Zambezi was out of sight before I jumped back into the water, swimming back towards the direction we came from in the way Zambezi taught me. I needed answers and had to figure out a way to get the symbol off me. How could a man protect me and I not fall for him? If I had to be honest with myself, I fell for Zambezi the first time I saw him.

# Sabrina

"**U**GHHHH!" I woke up choking on water. My pillow was wet, and my heart was beating uncontrollably. The nightmares I'd been having for many years were getting worse and causing me to drink.

"They're not real, Sabrina. The water people aren't real," I said to myself.

I stumbled out of bed, almost tripping over a pair of shoes from being light-headed. Often times I wondered where I came from and what family did I belong to. There were so many things I couldn't share with Shore because I wanted her life to be as least complicated as possible. I had a big case of memory loss. I'd searched hospital records and came up empty-handed. I had no real identity. The only thing I remembered about my past was waking up on the beach while pregnant. I was homeless and had to steal in order to survive after Shore was born. Along the way, I developed a drinking problem. When I went into the kitchen, there was a note on the table from Shore.

*How long did I sleep for?*

The watch on my wrist read nine o'clock. I slept a little over twelve hours. The fish Shore left on the table were staring at me with those small beady eyes. When I picked up the bowl, it glowed, lighting up the cabin.

"A male and a female angelfish."

*I remember these from somewhere. They're gifted when two souls are meant to be. Why does Shore have these? No, this is impossible, but my nightmares seemed to be coming true.*

I grabbed the fish bowl and ran out the cabin to set them free. If they were a gift to Shore, it meant she found her soul mate. My daughter was all I had. Why would anyone want to take her from me? Without her, I don't think I would survive.

I tossed the fish bowl into the lake and watched it sink before going back into the cabin. My purse sat on the kitchen floor. I stared at for a while, contemplating on if I wanted to drink the jar of moonshine I had inside. Shore wanted me to get better, I had to get better, but it was so hard.

*Okay, maybe I can do this one last time.*

I reached underneath the table to grab the moonshine out of my purse. When I sat back up, I dropped the jar and it shattered on the floor. Sitting across from me was a blurry silhouette made out of water. The presence sat the fish bowl back onto the table. It was a spirit. I couldn't move and the lighting inside the cabin dulled. The silhouette began changing. Seconds later, a woman with blueish green long hair was sitting across from me. Her hair was so long, it wrapped around the small table. Her long black nail twirled inside the fish bowl. She spoke words to them in another language as they swam around; she was playing with them.

"I don't think Shore would appreciate you treating these beautiful fish like trash," she said.

"You're not real."

"My dearest sister. What a waste to forget such a beautiful life. We had so much fun together. Pity you don't remember me. Why did you change your name?" she asked. I didn't have a name. When I was homeless with Shore, I went to a church. I told them I was a battered and homeless woman, so I could have shelter. They helped me change my identity, so I couldn't be found.

"I didn't have a name."

She banged on the table, her nails scratched the wood, almost splitting it in half.

"The water gave you life, Oceana. Now look at you. You kept Shore away from the waters and it made her sick! You've turned wicked," she said.

"I kept her safe!"

"You kept her human! How dare you drink that poison and pretend I don't exist. You've hurt us, Oceana. You hurt your own sister, but I will not let you take away from Shore's life again. She accepted her fate and maybe you should, too," she replied.

"Why do you keep coming to me? What do you want from me?"

"Nothing anymore. I only want you to let Shore live freely. Get her to know the waters.

She's growing and has desires now, the same as you did when you were younger. Since you cannot protect her anymore, Zambezi will," she said. She stood up and looked down at me.

"Shore is a princess now. Too bad the queen doesn't know her strength. When you fall back in love with the waters again, you will remember who you are. I cannot show you anymore because you drink poison when I do," she said.

"Please, just get out."

"You named me Jewel because you said I was the prettiest thing that came from the reef. Shore reminds me of you very much. Hopefully her ways can remind you of yourself, too. Just open your eyes before it's too late," Jewel said. When she disappeared, there was a puddle in the middle of the kitchen area. It slipped through the cracks in the floor of the cabin and just like that she disappeared. I don't remember anything of what she was talking about. The dreams I had weren't making any sense. It was like putting a puzzle together with the same pieces.

I went into the cupboard for another bottle of liquor I kept stashed away for emergencies.

*Why am I listening to a spirit anyway? Shore will not be with a boy until she's older. How would she handle a heart break? She's never experienced any of those things.*

The warm brown liquor soothed my throat while giving me a rush. Tears fell from my eyes, splashing loudly against the floor. There was an empty space in my heart. I had an amazing daughter but the emptiness inside was swallowing me, making me lose myself. The door to the cabin opened and Shore walked in naked and wet. I'd tried to ignore the changes of her body but there was something different about her. Maybe what the spirit said was true. Shore was a part of the waters.

"I thought you were going to quit," she said. Her eyes glowed; they were the same color as the reef I had dreams of. I fell onto the floor and burst into tears.

"You're possessed!"

"What?" she asked, rushing to me.

"Were you with that boy again?"

"Zambezi?" she asked.

"I'm not perfect, God knows that I'm not, but you are. This place is turning you. I thought it was going to bring us closer together but it's ripping us apart."

"Are you one of us? Why am I like this?" she asked.

I reached for the half-empty bottle of liquor and Shore snatched it away from me.

"I'm sick, too, baby. Your mother has been sick for a very long time. I see things the same as you. None of this is real. Don't give in."

"For a long time, I thought you had a drinking problem because of my illness and taking care of me by yourself. But you drink because you're afraid to realize the water people are real. You're hiding from something. Be honest with me, was my father human? Why do you see the water spirits if you're supposed to be human? You've been lying to me. Tell me the truth. What made you come here, to this lake?" she asked. It was a conversation I wasn't ready to have with Shore, but she wasn't a little girl anymore. Her mind was no longer naïve as she put the pieces together.

I stood off the floor and sat at the kitchen table, clutching the bottle of liquor in my hand. Shore sat across from me.

"I only lied to you to protect you from whatever it was I ran from. The story about your father isn't real. Honestly, I don't remember your father. I woke up on a beach, naked and wounded. There were three deep gashes in my legs. I could barely walk. Maybe it was from a shark but someone or something tried to hurt me. I couldn't bring myself to tell my sick child that I didn't know her father. Anyway, you loved hearing about your father and how much he loved you. For some reason, I thought you weren't going to live long. So many times, you had seizures that almost took you away from me. I couldn't let you leave this world thinking your father abandoned you because I don't know where he's at or who he is. I have no memory of him. I received a letter a month ago from an anonymous person. The letter stated that I should come to this place to find out what happened to me and there was a doctor who could help you. Inside the envelope with the letter was a map of how to get here. I couldn't tell you why we were coming, I figured you wouldn't fuss about it if you thought this place was connected to your father. It was the only way."

"I had a feeling you were lying to me. And I understand why you felt the need to protect me, but I don't think you can anymore because you live in denial. If you hadn't picked up a drinking addiction, you would have had all the answers you're looking for. You're still running from whatever it is that washed you up on shore. The only way we can change this is if you stop drinking and see the truth," she said.

"Stay away from that boy. I don't want you to end up raising a child alone."

I picked up my liquor bottle and left the cabin. The lake was a pretty blue with green specs. I sat on the rock Shore liked to sit on during the day to finish what was left of the bottle. After I chugged the rest of the liquor down, I threw the bottle into the lake. The bushes rustled behind me when I turned. A pair of red eyes were staring at me.

"Get the hell away from this property before I get my shotgun!"

The figure disappeared, and I burst into a fit of laughter.

"Come back again so I can blow a hole in your ass!"

I slid off the rock and stumbled back into the house. Shore was fixing tomato sandwiches. I almost fell over on the chair when I sat. She was disappointed in me.

"Maybe you don't need me anymore since those water people possessed you. They took you away from me."

"You're drunk and talking nonsense," she said with her back towards me.

"Now they have you disrespecting your mother. What's next? Are you going to leave and be with them?"

Shore placed my sandwich in front of me with a glass of water. Instead of sitting down with me, she went into her bedroom and slammed the door. The lake was turning my daughter against me. I had to figure out a way to move back into the city, so my precious angel could be normal again.

*Don't worry, Shore. I'm going to protect you and get you away from here. I thought this place was going to save you, but it changed you. I'll get more money soon then once I'm done, I'm going to burn this cabin down to the ground.*

# Zambezi

"**B**ro, you gotta look for Shore," Bay said when I tied the fishing boat to the dock. Shore was gone when me and Bay came to the boat after closing the market. She was being too dramatic when all I wanted to do was protect her feelings. She was too pure—innocent for me to corrupt her.

"I'm sure she's home."

"But she just learned how to swim, bro. How do you know she's safe?" he asked.

"Yo, why in the fuck are you sweating me? Shore is good! The fuck you want me to do, stop conducting business to chase behind some whiny-ass water fairy?"

Bay got off the boat and grabbed his cooler. I didn't mean to raise my voice at him, but I couldn't focus under pressure.

"Look, bro. My bad for yelling at you. I'm stressed out right now. I can't get Shore out of my head. The shit is bothering me."

"So, you're feeling her?" he asked as we headed towards the woods.

"Yeah, but I don't want a relationship right now. Shore is relationship material, the kind where you bring her flowers and things like that. You know I like to bounce afterwards but with her, I'm gonna have to catch her some seashells and all that dainty stuff water fairies like."

"You got a point. Sooo, can I date her?" Bay asked.

"Naw, bro. You ain't a man yet. What about your girlfriend?"

"What about her? I'm ready to break up with her. Her and her sister just have the looks, but lack brain activity like an oyster," Bay chuckled.

When we made it to the cabin, Adwoa was sitting in front the house, burning those pungent-smelling candles again. She had a scowl on her face because it was ten o'clock at night, thirty minutes past Bay's curfew.

"You have my son out too late," Adwoa said.

"He's not a baby."

Adwoa walked down the cabin steps with the candle in her hand. She threw hot wax in Bay's face. Tears stung the brim of his eyes, but he didn't let them fall. Instead, he remained still, preparing for more punishment.

"You will not be like your brother and be intimate with humans," Adwoa yelled, pointing her sharp nail into Bay's face. She raised her hand to slap him, but I grabbed her arm, almost snatching it out of socket.

"You raise your hand again and I'm going to bite your head off your neck! Bay is your son, he's not your mate!" My father stormed out of the house, his eyes turning into the color of his creature's. Fish scales and reptile-like skin covered his body. Thick locs grew from his scalp and his heavy feet shook the ground beneath.

"Father, no!" Bay yelled out when he knocked me into a tree. He was protecting Adwoa. I wasn't angry that he came to her defense, I was pissed off because he didn't come to Bay's. Adwoa was abusive to us for many years and he allowed her to be. He grabbed me around the throat, his over-sized hands slamming me into a tree, almost crushing my back.

"Punish him, Caspian!" Adwoa yelled.

"I told you to never disrespect my mate again!" his deep voice bellowed throughout the woods. My necklace shielded me, burning my father's hands.

"I don't want to fight you, Father, but I will fuckin' kill you if you touch me again!"

"Take that necklace off!" he yelled. Bay snatched a small tree out of the ground and hit my father in the legs with it.

"Get off of him!" Bay shouted.

I bit a chunk out of my father's neck and blood squirted into the ground as he dropped to his knees. Adwoa ran to him and applied pressure to his neck.

"I want you off my property tonight!" my father gasped while turning into his human form.

"What happened to my father, Adwoa? Why is he so weak?"

My father was supposed to heal from the wound on his neck, but the wound was still bleeding out. The man that laid on the ground in front of me wasn't one of the leaders of the sea. It seemed as if he was more human than creature.

"What did you do to him, Adwoa? Why hasn't my father healed yet?"

"Maybe because you're too dangerous now," she said, helping him up. Bay was confused, he didn't know whose side to take. Adwoa gave birth to him and we only shared a father.

"Help your father inside the cabin," Adwoa said to Bay. Bay looked at me for confirmation and I nodded, telling him to help our father. Bay walked him into the cabin, leaving a trail of blood behind.

"Your mother was wicked and that necklace you have of hers is wicked, too. This can all go away if you believe in the god I praise. Give in, Zambezi and let my god heal your spirit. You have a lot of hate and darkness inside you. My candles cannot keep the darkness away from this cabin," she said.

"Your god is trash, Adwoa. You are trash, too. You've done something to my father and I will figure it out. The darkness around here lives within you. There must be a reason why I can't get inside your head. You might have the waters flowing through your veins, but you are not a part of them."

"Soon, your father will be drained then I'll need another flesh in my bed. You're getting stronger. You'll be able to take his place, but you won't be able to if you don't take off that necklace," she stated.

"My father will figure you out soon enough," I replied, walking away.

"I can smell that girl on you! Stay your ass away from her or else this small town will flood with blood!" Adwoa called out. I didn't want to go inside my cabin and was too exhausted to get a hotel room in the inner-city. I'd have to take my boat almost two hours out. My feet had a mind of their own because they were heading towards Lake Deep.


**\*\*\*\*\*\*\*\*\*\***


Shore's cabin was quiet. The lake had a beautiful glow at night, reminding me of the visions I had of the Mediterranean Sea, where my father migrated from. We lived in a secluded cave that was hidden off shore when I was a baby. Which is the reason I named my market, The Shore. Meeting Shore wasn't just a coincidence.

A small flicker came through the inside of her bedroom, perhaps from a candle. I moved quietly so I wouldn't wake up her mother. Shore was sitting up in her bed, wearing a pajama shirt. Her teal curls covered her eyes; when she moved her hair behind her ear, I saw tears. She hugged herself, while rocking back and forth. Her pecan skin glistened from the candle's reflection. Her meaty thighs looked subtle—delicate. She jumped, almost knocking over a nightstand when I tapped the window, beckoning her to come outside. She lifted up the window, and leaned over with her arms crossed, giving me attitude.

"Why did you leave?" I asked while wiping her tears away.

"Because I wanted to practice my swimming. What are you doing here?" she asked.

"Just taking a walk."

"Is that blood on you?" she asked.

"Yeah, I got into it with my father. What's up with you? Why are you crying?"

"My mother upsets me sometimes. She's a good woman but she holds a lot back from me. She also drinks so much that I don't know if she's aware of reality," she replied.

"Come take a walk with me."

"It's almost midnight. The town is sleeping," she replied.

"So, you shoot me down when I wanna talk but get mad at me when I don't give you enough attention? Make up your mind, beautiful. Besides, the night is young."

"Only because I need some fresh air. This isn't about you, okay?" she asked.

"Whatever you say."

Shore grabbed her flip-flops and handed them to me. She threw her leg over the sill and I caught a slight glimpse of her pussy. I should've turned my head but being around me with no panties on was going to wake the monster. She was moving slowly, careful not to make a sound. I grabbed her by the hips and pulled her out the window.

"You didn't have to do all that!" she whispered.

"Come on sea turtle," I said, grabbing her hand. She snatched away from me and playfully pushed me in the chest.

"Where are we going?" she asked. Shore slipped her hand back into mine and I looked at it for a second. When I grabbed her hand, it was to get her to move faster. She took it as a romantic gesture, but I couldn't pull away. Her small, soft hand got lost in my palm.

"I've always wanted to do this. Even wrote in my diary about it," she said.

"Wanted to do what?"

"Take long walks with someone while holding hands. That's childish, isn't it?" she giggled.

"Naw, it's sorta different. I'm not much of a talker though. I get straight down to the point."

"You mean you fuck first then ask questions later?" She frowned her nose.

"I wouldn't have worded it like that but yeah. What's the point of connecting with someone when you can't be yourself around them? All of the women I've been with were human. Do you think they'll love me if they know I'm a big-ass water creature?"

"What about Laguna? What is she?"

"She's human, but she thinks she's a water fairy. She doesn't know they really exist, but she goes by the tales she heard. She just worships them. So, I've never been with someone from the waters," I replied.

"Interesting. Men never date people who understand them. Instead, they go outside the box," she said.

"It's cool to have balance. Sometimes I want to escape what I am to seem normal. We have to accept that more humans are mortal than immortal. This is their world now, we're outnumbered, so we can't truly be ourselves."

"Where are we going?" she asked. We were ten minutes away from her cabin.

"There is a small cave deep inside the woods where the lake flows through. I used to go there a lot when I was younger, because it reminded me so much of the visions I have. Adwoa stopped me from going so I haven't gone in years because I lost touch with it. Now I feel like visiting."

"Does it have something to do with the fight you had with your father?" she asked.

"He attacked me because I grabbed Adwoa's arm. She burned Bay's face with a candle because he missed his curfew. That bitch is crazy. I want to kill her, but she's my brother's mother. Tonight, something came inside me that I've never felt. Just a lot of built-up anger."

"I guess we're both having issues at home," she said.

"Your mother loves you. She's protecting you from the world."

"I'll protect you," Shore said.

I was looking forward to a giggle, the same as she did after she told a joke or was sarcastic.

"You don't even know me like that."

"I don't have to know you to know you'd do the same for me. Besides, look at it like this. We're best friends now," she said while lifting up my shirt.

"We do have matching tattoos, huh?"

"Yeah," she smiled.


Fifteen minutes later, we were at the cave. Shore was skeptical about it at first because it was dark inside, but the glow from the lake gave it light.

"I won't let nothing happen to you."

"It just looks so out of place from this town," she said, peeking inside.

I pulled her into the cave and she squeezed my hand, digging her nails into my skin. She must not have realized how sharp her nails were. A school of fish followed Shore as she walked alongside of the water.

"It's beautiful in here. Reminds me of the vacation commercials of tropical caves. The sounds of the water are soothing. I can sleep here," she said.

"I found it during a storm. Me and Bay were swimming at the bottom of the lake, looking for fish. The storm pulled me away from home and I ended up here."

There was a spot inside the cave where I used to rest and think a lot. The bed of moss was bigger since the last time I'd seen it. The moss stretched alongside of the cave's wall. Shore sat down and placed her feet inside the water. Fish swam around her legs, tickling her.

"How deep is the water below?" she asked.

"Like fifty feet. Maybe more since it rained heavily over the years."

Shore's legs turned into a fish tail; she flapped it, splashing water everywhere.

"You can control it now."

"It happens when I'm nervous more so," she blushed.

I took off my shoes to put my feet in the water. Scales covered my legs and arms. Shore stared at me for a while, observing me.

"You have locs in the water. Why is that?" she asked.

"My father told me it was to protect my head."

Shore rested her head on my shoulder and her hair smelled like fruit. Her skin against mine was giving me an erection.

"Can I taste you?" I heard myself say. Shore lifted up her head, looking at me with confusion.

*Why in the fuck did I say that out loud?*

"I didn't mean it like that. That came out wrong. You just smell so good and my mind slipped to someplace else." Shore was making me nervous. All the tough talk was gone. It was just me and her inside a cave with nobody stopping us from doing whatever we wanted. Her tail shrank then disappeared. She got up and walked away from the water. Shore went into a corner and crossed her arms. I pissed her off again.

"What did I do this time?"

"Nothing at all," she said.

"You're a virgin, Shore. It seems to me you want me to fuck you or something. Is this how you want someone to deflower you? Don't you want it to be special?"

"Of course, I want it to be special but that's not the problem. You send mixed signals and I don't understand them. It feels like I'm throwing myself at you when all I want is for you to see that I like you," she replied.

"I like you, too. You're the only person who can come here. And, besides, I told you a few things about myself that I don't speak on. This situation is fucking with me also because you don't need someone like me."

"You can change if you want to. What's stopping you?" she asked.

"I'm not ready to."

"What kind of tasting were you referring to?" she asked, putting me on the spot.

"You know what I was talking about."

"What's stopping you?" she asked.

I've never come across a virgin, but I assumed they shied away from sex. She wanted to feel a man's touch, she was craving it. We both had an appetite for each other, but it would've been wrong for me to enter her. I had no right to that part of her. I took off my bloody shirt and tossed it onto the ground. Shore eyed my chest, she was aroused. Her nipples were pressed against the material of her shirt and her eyes glowed, matching the water of the cave. I no longer had the upper-hand. True, I might have been more experienced in being intimate, but Shore had outdone me. She was calling my bluff, testing me. Giving me options that she had not given another man. I kneeled in front of her and she trembled from nervousness when I gently grabbed her neck. Her breathing deepened.

"You don't run shit, Shore."

"I think you want me to," she replied.

I brought her lips closer to mine then kissed her. Her soft lips almost made my dick explode. If kissing had always felt that way, I would've been a one-woman man. She froze when I grabbed her soft breasts. She moaned loudly, and the scent of her arousal caused a low, deep grunt. While exploring her mouth, my hands went below her waist. Shore held her legs open when I buried my fingers into her hips, pulling her underneath me. She closed her eyes when I touched her fat wet mound. The heat from between her legs was like a sauna. She covered her eyes when I kissed her inner-thighs.

"Do you want me to stop?"

"No," she trembled.

When I moved her shirt away, her pussy stared at me. Shore's clit wasn't a normal clit; hers was the color of an oyster's pearl. Her nails dug into my shoulders when I kissed her pussy and a deep gasp slipped from her lips.

*Maybe this will cure her need for sex.*

# Shore

Zambezi's tongue felt better than what I dreamt. He was turning, but not completely. His arms changed and his locs were draped over my thighs. His tongue pierced through my slit and I covered my mouth. My legs clamped on him and he pried them away. I looked around for something to grab but couldn't find anything. I grabbed his hair to keep him steady. The pressure his tongue applied inside of me was making my head spin.

"Zammbezzziiii, nooooooo!" I cried out.

His tongue vibrated inside of me, causing my body to shake. With his free hand, he rubbed my clit. The tingling sensation along with more pressure, made my pussy squirt. I wanted him to stop because I wasn't expecting that kind of pleasure. Zambezi's tongue was buried deep inside of me. He pulled my clit between his lips, French kissing my mound afterwards. His tongue vibrated on my clit and I wondered how it was possible. More essence squirted out of me as I screamed out in pleasure. My inner-thighs were sweaty, and my hair stuck to the nape of my neck. His growls were husky, but they weren't the kind of growls that came from a dog. His huffs were of an extremely big animal. I couldn't help stuffing my shirt into my mouth when he used his thumb to massage my anus. Sounds of him lapping up my wetness echoed throughout the cave. Seconds later, Zambezi pulled away from me, leaving me drained. His face was drenched in my fluids. He used the end of my shirt to wipe his face off. I cringed, wondering if he would be mad at me but then he smiled.

"Was that supposed to happen?"

"Yeah, I'd have to question you if it didn't. It's a gift to get wet like that," he chuckled. The butterflies I had were making my stomach hurt, I was nauseous. Zambezi laid next to me and pulled me towards him. One of his arms cradled me, the other was behind my head as a pillow. He massaged my scalp and my eyes grew heavy. My legs were still twitching, and my pussy still throbbed. His mouth was away from me yet I was still having an orgasm.

"What did you do to me?" I asked while my nectar dripped down my legs. A puddle formed underneath me.

"I did what you wanted to do. It'll stop soon," he said.

"It's still coming from your tongue?"

"My kind used their tongue to send signals to each other back in time. The vibration created sound waves. I guess we can use it for other things now," he said.

"Make it stop!"

Seconds later, my back lifted off the ground and soft wails mixed with cries of pleasure filled the cave while another orgasm rippled through my tunnel. It was stronger than the last few. Zambezi rubbed my clit and sucked on my neck as my hips bucked forward, forcing me to hump the air. My body was like a noodle, moving in ways that it never moved before.

"Pleasssseeee, get it out of me! Whatever you did to me, make it go away!"

"Ssshhhhh," he whispered into my ear. He took my breasts into his mouth, causing my nipples to insanely ache from vibration. My nipples were sensitive when he massaged them, pressing his fingers into my flesh. I almost fainted. The orgasm was still building up, it was at its peak.

"This is the big wave, beautiful," he said.

It was rising, causing my clit to swell into the size of a grape. My nipples expanded, swollen from the pressure. My legs caught a cramp and I could barely catch my breath. Zambezi covered my mouth and held me closer while I came. My wetness saturated the moss underneath us. My knees buckled while ferociously humping the air. My moans, grunts and cries were muffled. Tears of pleasure drenched my face and my shirt was ruined from sweat and my essence squirting everywhere. My body went still after the vibration stopped. Zambezi uncovered my mouth and moved the hair out of my face. He kissed my lips again and I was too tired to kiss him back. My eyelids were getting heavier while trying to fight sleep. I couldn't stay awake any longer...

\*\*\*\*\*\*\*\*\*\*\*

I woke up to the sounds of different voices shouting. For a moment, I thought I was dreaming about me and Zambezi being intimate inside a tropical cave, but it was all real. He was standing in front of me, his deep voice shouting at someone. He wasn't in human form and a gold shield-like underwear covered his butt. He was taller, his head almost touching the top of the cave. His back was covered in gold snake-like skin. He had the same kind of skin on his calves which had sharp blades the shape of fins. If I didn't know any better, he was in defense mode. His voice dripped with anger and his shoulders looked tense. I got up and stood beside him. There were eight water fairies in the water, but one of them was standing on the ground in human form. Her wild and long kinky hair was jet-black with green highlights. Her hair covered her private parts. She had an umber complexion with ocean blue eyes. The seashell charm bracelet on her wrist looked familiar.

"Rain?" I asked.

"Welcome home," she smiled.

"So, you know her?" Zambezi asked.

"Yeah, sorta. Why are you arguing with them?"

"She was hovered over us while we were sleeping. She said she wanted to take you in the water. I can't send you with strangers. I'm supposed to protect you," Zambezi said.

"She's one of us! We won't hurt her," Rain said.

"Why in the fuck were you creeping on us then?" Zambezi asked. The water fairies splashed Zambezi with their tails. I covered my mouth to keep myself from laughing. He was annoyed, but they only wanted to have fun.

"Where is my mirror?" a water fairy with pink hair asked.

"Stop being selfish, Reef. She'll get you one soon. Don't mind her, she likes looking at herself all day," Rain said. Rain walked over to me and pulled me into a hug. It'd been years, but she was still the same person with a bubbly attitude.

"I know I'm late. Seems like I'm the last one to see you, but when my mother, Giva, told me you were coming, I went searching for the best seashells I could find. I've been feeling guilty for a long time because I lured you into the waves, but Jewel ordered me to," Rain said. Zambezi stepped away and the water fairies teased him.

"Servant," one said.

"Fuck all of y'all," he replied.

"We heard your moans last night. Tell me, is it as big as it looks?" someone asked me.

"Let's have some respect for Shore's mate!" Rain said.

"Well, sisters do share information. I've heard serpents have snake dicks and if that is true, our sister should stay away from him," Reef said.

"Ohhhhkayyyy."

"Well, is it big? The sisters want to know because human dicks aren't completing me anymore. Does he have a brother we can have?" another fairy said.

"He's the offspring of Caspian," Reef whispered to someone. Reef and Rain looked almost identical. I wondered if they were both Giva's daughters.

"Reef don't give them the fuel," Rain said.

"Why do you think you can boss me around? You came here to bring her bracelet, but we followed because we heard moans coming from this cave. We want to hear the story," Reef replied.

"Just tell them so they can leave," Zambezi said while pulling his hair back.

"I'm sorry I don't feel comfortable," I told them.

"Maybe some other time. Nothing to see here, sisters. Let's get ready for the club tonight," Reef said. They went underneath the water and disappeared.

"Y'all go to clubs, too?"

"Well, some of us like to feel the land and then most of us don't like to leave the waters. We can talk another time, I'll be at the market with Reef later. I'll meet you there," Rain said.

"Okay, we can catch up then."

"Wait, I came to give you this. It matches the one I have," Rain said. She grabbed my arm and tied the seashell charm bracelet around my wrist. The bracelet was a little heavy, but I loved it. I thanked her, and she hugged me again before jumping into the water, to join the others.

"That was interesting."

"Tell me about it. I've heard stories of water fairies being very sexual and trouble makers, but I didn't think it was true until now. Seems like your kind isn't as innocent as you appear," Zambezi said.

"Excuse me?"

"I'm just saying, soon you'll be like them. Your innocence will be gone," he said.

"I'm still my own person."

"Are you ready to head back? I have to go to my father's market today," he said.

"Cool."

We made small talk on our way back to the cabin, but Zambezi was more quiet than usual. I wanted to get inside his head the same way he does me, but I didn't know how to.

"Did I do something wrong?" I asked when we made it back to my cabin.

"Naw, I just got a lot on my mind right now. I have to go home and face my father after what happened last night. We will talk later. I'll be back in an hour, and we can go to the market together," he said. Zambezi kissed my cheek before he walked away. I didn't go into the cabin until I saw him disappear into the woods. It was morning and I hoped my mother was asleep when I snuck in. The cabin was quiet and spotless.

*She must've cleaned up after I snuck out.*

I walked into my bedroom and my bed was made up with a note on the pillow. The note read:

*I'm going into the city to seek counseling for my addiction. I'll return when I'm ready to be the parent you need me to be. I wanted to kiss you goodbye, but you weren't in your bed. I have a feeling you were with that boy, but you're grown now. You'll be twenty-one soon. I was your age when I had you so be careful with that boy and protect yourself. I'm sick, Shore—very sick. I realized how much I have been hurting you over the years last night so I'm going to fix it. I left you some money underneath the floorboard by your window. But in the meantime, be free. Spread your wings and don't let me keep you from living. Get a job if you want to. I love you very much!*

I sat on the bed and stared at the letter. There were dried wet spots that smeared some of the ink from my mother. She was crying while writing the letter. I couldn't force myself to cry because I wasn't sad. If anything, I was happy for her. She was an alcoholic with a troubled past. Knowing that she was seeking help was a relief because she wanted to better herself for us. I placed the letter on my dresser next to my fish bowl. When I got a closer look at them, I noticed something was off about the male fish. The female fish swam around him to get his attention, but he ignored her.

*Do they feel what me and Zambezi feel?*

I touched the male fish and he rammed his head into my finger. He wanted me out of his bowl.

"Okay, fine! Be mad, jackass!"

I grabbed my things for a bath. Seeing Rain again excited me, remembering what it was like to have a friend even though it was only for a split second. Looking at the clock on the wall, I realized I only had thirty minutes to bathe and get dressed.

## Two hours later...

Zambezi didn't come back so I had to walk to town myself. The long dirt road seemed to be never-ending. The sun was scorching hot, but I managed to keep cool by walking in the shade alongside the trees. While walking, I couldn't stop thinking about my mother. I truly hoped she was serious about getting the help she needed. When I made it to town, people were out on the sidewalks with their stands. The small stores were crowded and there was a line outside of Zambezi's family market. There was a group of girls standing outside the ice cream shop. I counted about ten of them, they all had different colored hair and were dressed flashy. They were the center of the town. The one wearing a sleeveless romper and stilettos turned around; it was Rain. She waved me over and I joined them.

"Wow, I didn't know all of that was underneath that shirt," Reef said, referring to my shorts. I didn't look as flashy as them. Matter of fact, I felt out of place. They were all beautiful: some were slim, medium and curvy like me in size.

"We'll meet you all at the jewelry store," Rain told the girls. They waved at me before walking off. Rain and Reef were the only two who stayed back.

"I just want you to know Zambezi walked into the market with that big-head girl, Laguna. Do you want me to fight her? Just say the word," Reef said. Reef was wearing jean shorts with a lace camisole. Her pink hair was styled in cornrows going back.

"Why do you always want to fight people from this town?" Rain laughed.

"You know this town is cursed," Reef whispered.

"What do you mean?" I replied.

"They say the people here worship a demon. They are normal by day and wicked by night. That's why the stores close early," Reef said.

"That's because they are farmers and have to go bed early for work," Rain said.

"Mother said they were," Reef said.

"Our mother is spiritual, everything is wicked to her but if it is, Shore can fix it," Rain said.

"What makes you think I can fix anything?" I asked.

"You wear your mother's locket. The locket shows things that we can't see," Rain said.

"What does my mother have to do with it?"

"Your mother is our queen, but Jewel took her spot. Jewel is strong, but your mother was stronger. Without her, the waters slowly suffer, leaving it open for water demons," Rain said.

"She didn't tell me that. Now I'm wondering if she left because she's running from what she is, instead of trying to get help."

"We're still your family and you have us. If she stays gone too long, we'll help you find her. But maybe she needs the time away to think clearly,"

Rain said. I wasn't feeling any better because I had a feeling my mother was running away from me. Here I was caught up in Zambezi while my mother was going through something.

"You can stay with us at the beach house," Reef said.

"You all live in a beach house?"

"It's abandoned but we live there. Jewel would love for you to come. She was waiting for you to get comfortable, so we wouldn't scare you," Rain said.

"I'll just visit in case my mother comes back."

"Let's go to the market for fresh lemonade," Reef said.

We walked into Zambezi's father's market and it was crowded. Bay was carrying a fish net over his shoulder with a lot of fish inside. He gave me a head nod before walking up the stairs. Reef nudged me, telling me to look behind me. Zambezi and Laguna were talking in front of a fresh vegetable stand. Zambezi had a smirk on his face while Laguna was touching on his arms. She wrapped his arms around her waist, but he didn't pull away until he saw me staring at him.

"The disrespect! He likes humans anyway," Rain said, and Reef agreed.

"Let's get mother's oranges then we can go," Rain said.

I rolled my eyes at Zambezi while Reef pulled me away.

"So, we're going to the club tonight. You'll have so much fun. One of our sisters dances tonight," Reef said.

"A stripper?"

"More so an erotic dancer," Rain said.

"Girl, that hoe a stripper," Reef laughed, and Rain rolled her eyes.

"Why do you embarrass us? Mother would whip you with a switch if she heard you and she's not a hoe. Lake is just loving nature and the things that live in it," Rain said.

"Isn't that a hoe?" Reef asked me.

"Yes, but who are we to judge?"

Rain and Reef got a few things for their mother and Jewel before we left the market. We met up with the rest of the fairies and one of them gifted me a necklace and a summer dress.

"We always give each other gifts," Rain said.

*Shore, turn around,* Zambezi's voice came into my head. He was standing in the entryway of the market. Looking at his tall frame and muscled arms brought back the feeling I had at the cave. He waved me over to him and I turned back around.

"He's coming over here," Rain whispered.

"Can I talk to you for a second?" Zambezi asked when he approached me. The fairies surrounded him, and he threw his hands up in frustration.

"So, what y'all short asses gonna jump me or sumthin?" Zambezi chuckled.

"I haven't fought a man in a while, but I can take him," one of the fairies said. There were a lot of them and I couldn't remember their names.

"Y'all ain't doing shit to me," Zambezi said.

He grabbed my hand and pulled me away from them. I signaled that I was fine, and they backed away from us.

"You don't need my protection anymore since you have them. So, this is how it's gonna be now? I got to go through them to talk to you?" he asked.

"I see you and Laguna have rekindled."

"You trippin' over that? That's not about nothing. I owe you this for helping me out yesterday morning. I'll be by tomorrow to start working on your cabin," he said. Zambezi pulled money out of his pocket and placed it inside my hand.

"Go ahead and get back to your friends. I'll see you around," he said and walked away. While I was putting the money into my pocket, someone bumped me. The money fell out of my hand and someone snatched it off the ground. It was Laguna.

"You will not be taking money from my man!" she said with her four friends standing behind her.

"Give it back or I'm gonna whip your fuckin' ass!"

"Ohhhh, I'm scared. You think because you come from the outside I'm supposed to fear your ghetto, poor ass? Let me tell you something, my family helped build this town so therefore I run it. Zambezi belongs to me and you're going to stay away from him or else I'll burn that insect-infested cabin down to the ground. You owe me this money for even looking at my man!" Laguna said. I reached for the money and she slapped me. It was the final straw. I jumped on her and slammed my fist into her face. Her friends stood back and watched because they were outnumbered. Laguna screamed for someone to help her, but I couldn't stop hitting her. My nails were like fishing hooks as they pierced through her skin. People from the town pulled me away from her. Laguna laid on the sidewalk crying because I cut her neck and arms.

"You need to get out of this town!" one of her friends said to me.

"These are our waters and we'll go wherever the fuck they are!" Rain shouted at her while Reef held her back.

"Let's just go!" I told them.

We walked away from them while the people in the town cursed us. Rain was still upset and yelling back at them.

"We were here before all of you and soon we'll be the last ones standing! Mark my words, shitholes, we aren't going anywhere!" Rain screamed.

"And everyone thinks I'm the crazy one," Reef said, handing me my money.

"See, this is why we barley come to the markets. Those people look at us because we're different. Our ancestors were here before humans existed, they have been here since Earth was born," Rain said.

"Look what I have," Lake said, waving Laguna's Louis Vuitton hand bag.

"Let me see that!" someone said, snatching it away from Lake.

"This is fake," she said, throwing Laguna's bag on the ground.

"You really think her and her friends go shopping? They're a bunch of fakes," Rain said. We walked down the long dirt road, heading towards my cabin. The fairies talked and bragged about the ass whipping Laguna received. I couldn't wait to get out of my clothes. Laguna's blood was smeared across my white shirt, but if I could do it all over again, I would.

**Two hours later….**

We were on an old school bus, heading towards the city. Rain passed me a blunt and a small gold bottle that was decorated with diamonds.

"What is this?"
"It's wine, we make it ourselves. Taste it," she said. I sniffed the bottle and the smell was strong, almost like a dirty fish tank.

"This smell horrible."

"It's made out of natural ingredients with a mixture of coral reef snake blood. Don't worry, it won't kill you. It's better than drinking what the humans drink," Rain said. I took a sip of the pungent liquor and the taste was indescribable. There were small mushy chunks in the wine. I gagged and almost threw up.

"You'll get used to it. It's very nasty but it makes you feel good," Darya said. Darya was one of the quiet ones. She didn't talk much unless it was about weed or sea wine. She had a lighter skin than the rest of us and her burnt orange hair was bone straight. Darya's father was Native American, and her mother was from the sea.

"So, ladies, the plan is to wear something sexy tonight. First impressions are lasting impressions," Lake said.

"What's special about tonight besides the club?" I asked.

"Male water fairies will be there. If you noticed, we don't have any male fairies in our waters," Rain said.

"Why is that?"

"We just live differently. We only pair up for life if we have an offspring, but a lot of us are mating with humans. Let's just say they are the bachelors of the sea. The only time they migrate is if they're ready to reproduce and a few of our sisters are ready," she said.

"They're soooo whack," Reef said, filing her nails.

"Why would you say that?" Lake asked.

"Because I wanted to. Male fairies are weak, we're the ones who hunt, kill and protect our waters. All they do is give us babies. We're the dominant ones so that's why a lot of us are sleeping with humans. Sorry to burst your bubble, but I'm not protecting my mate. He's supposed to protect me!" Reef said.

"They are very wealthy!" Lake yelled at Reef.

"It's all fine and dandy until a man touches your ass in front of him and he'll just sit there and sip his wine," Reef replied.

"You evil little bitch!" Lake yelled at Reef.

"Kick shells, bitch. I'm only going so I can use one of them as a bank but he's definitely not touching me. Just the thought of one makes me sick," Reef replied.

Lake got up and went to the front of the bus and Reef shrugged her shoulders.

"I hope you apologize," Rain said to Reef.

"I will in an hour," Reef replied.


Once we arrived in Germantown, Maryland, Pearl parked the bus inside a garage. Pearl was a little older than the rest of us; she didn't hang out with the girls, instead she drove them places and waited for them.

"Okay, girls. You have two hours to return back," she shouted as we got off the bus.

Everyone split up and went their separate ways. I stayed with Rain and Reef. Zambezi gave me six-hundred dollars from working at his market. I thought it was a bit too much for one day, but I was grateful. Reef wanted to go inside an urban clothing store. Rap music blared throughout the speakers inside the store and a teenage girl came over to us.

"Good evening, welcome to Urban Outfitters. Let us know if you need help finding anything," she said to us before walking away.

"Reef, you better not steal shit!" Rain whispered.

"Have some faith in your little sister," Reef said and scurried off.

"Do you like this?" I asked Rain.

"It'll look good on you," she said.

It was a white stretchy cotton dress with slits on the side. The only shoes I could imagine wearing with them were nude sandals with a heel. Rain picked up something similar, but her dress was black.

"When you have loud hair, it's hard to wear a lot of colors," she joked.

We were in the store for twenty minutes and I had everything I wanted which was six pieces of clothing. Reef and Rain had two shopping bags a piece. While strolling the strip of stores, I came across a small antique shop. Inside the window was a big mirror. The mirror had four legs. I went inside with Reef and Rain in tow. There was a short white woman behind the counter. She looked to be in her mid-sixties.

"Good evening. How can I help you?" she asked.

"How much is the mirror in the window?

"It's three-hundred dollars."

"That's too much," Rain whispered.

"Yeah, we appreciate it but save your money," Reef said.

"I'll tell you what. I can let you get it for half. You're the first person to come in here asking about it. It's been here for four years," she said.

"One thirty and we have a deal," Reef said, and Rain nudged her.

"One-thirty-five," the old woman said.

"I'll take it."

I went inside my small money bag and placed the money on the counter.

"Now, listen. I can't help you girls carry that mirror. It's made out of brass and steel. So, I hope you have strong backs," she said.

"Oh, we can do it," Rain said.

Rain and Reef picked up the mirror with ease. The old woman applauded. "It took four of my grandsons to carry that in and they barely made it," she said.

"We ate our seaweed growing up," Rain smiled.

We exited the shop, and I offered to help but they told me to carry the bags instead.

"Let's take these things to the bus then we can go to look for shoes," Reef suggested.

"Okay."

I was having a blast with the fairies. In just a short period of time, they taught me a lot. One thing was for sure, I felt so beautiful. People in the town couldn't stop staring at us and a few humans asked us about our skin and hair care routine. Memories of living in the hood was fading away and were being replaced by my life in Oland. I prayed my mother came back soon so I could share the happiness with her.

# Zambezi

**Meanwhile in Oland...**

The markets were closing. Bay and Cascade helped me get rid of seafood we couldn't sell because it had been out the water for over two days. We didn't freeze the fish, we kept them on cold ice. Cascade and Bay were talking about the fight with Laguna and Shore.

"Shore fucked Laguna up. Ara asked me why I didn't help out her sister. What the hell I look like fighting a woman?" Bay asked, and Cascade roared in laughter. I was the one to blame. Shore saw me talking to Laguna, but it was innocent, until Laguna caught Shore staring at us. Laguna purposely brushed up on me to piss Shore off.

"You need to dump, Ara, bro. She's an airhead," Cascade said.

"Can y'all stop gossiping and get to fucking work?"

"Bro, why are you always angry? Didn't you get some pussy last night?" Bay asked. Sometimes Bay's mind was immature because he thought everything was simple.

"Why do you think pussy solves everything? Hell, you should know that, ask your bitch-ass father." Bay slammed the box down on the floor.

"That's your father, too. If you don't want to work here, then leave! You have your own shit to worry about. Matter of fact, maybe my mother would have some peace if you didn't carry your troubles home," Bay seethed.

"The only reason why I'm here is because of you. Can you run this market by yourself? Be honest, cause the last time I checked, I been working in here since I was a little boy, while you were still drinking breast milk! Prove to me you're a man now and I'll leave this town and never look back!"

"Wooowwww, y'all chill out!" Cascade said.

"I'm out!"

I picked up my butcher's knife set and headed out the door. There were a few people walking down the sidewalk, but everyone else was returning home. I used to love Oland, but it didn't flow through my veins anymore. There was a disconnect between me and the market. I stood by my father's side, helping him serve the people. Tears burned the rims of my eyes, but they wouldn't fall. Sea dragons couldn't cry. No matter how much pain or sadness filled our hearts, the tears never fall.

Adwoa was sitting on the porch when I walked up the path to our territory. She was burning those candles and putting red paint on her face while chanting in an unfamiliar language.

"Can I see my father?" I asked, stepping on the porch.

"I heard Shore attacked someone today. You still think she's innocent?"

"Laguna brought that on herself, Adwoa. Now, excuse me while I check up on my father."

"He's in bed," she said.

I opened the screen door and entered their cabin. The home didn't have the fresh water scent it used to have, it smelled like death. The hallway was dark and cold. We didn't have air conditioning and it was summertime. The cabin should've been warm. My father was in bed with a bandage wrapped around his neck. His skin was pale and dead skin covered his lips. He weakly reached out to me and I kneeled next to him.

"I'm sorry, Father. I thought you were going to heal, and I was only defending myself."

"Help meeeee," he whispered.

Tears were falling from his bloodshot red eyes. My father was an immortal with a sick human's strength—it was unreal.

"What happened?"

"The candles are kil—"

He choked up blood and his eyes rolled to the back of his head. My father shook uncontrollably, fighting to breathe. I heard Adwoa running down the hallway. I picked up my father and tossed him over my shoulder.

"NOOOOOO!" Adwoa screamed when I jumped through the glass window.

"BRING HIM BACK!" she yelled.

My father was dehydrated. I couldn't remember the last time he swam in the lake. A knife went through my calf, but I kept running. I was a ways away from the lake, probably another ten minutes, even running as fast as I was going. Another knife pierced through my leg and I tumbled, keeping my balance. A sharper knife went through my back, piercing through my stomach. When I fell, my father's frail body went down a hill. Adwoa jumped on me, her sharp knife-like teeth tearing open my neck. I grabbed her by the neck and slammed her onto the ground. Her black eyes were soulless and her skin was gray with black spots. Adwoa's long locs were matted and she didn't have a nose.

*What is she? This isn't a water fairy.*

Since I was a little boy, I thought Adwoa was a water fairy even though I never saw her swimming in the lake. She had ways like a fairy and her beauty was alluring.

"His soul belongs to me and soon yours will, too," she said. She straddled me, grabbing at my dick. Suddenly, her screams pierced my ears after I blew water into her face, slicing her cheeks from the impact. She fell onto the ground, holding her bloody face.

"Kill me and you won't find a cure for your father,"she hissed. I pulled the knife out of my stomach and blood poured out of me, soaking the ground beneath me. While Adwoa laid on the ground, I rushed to my father. The fall down the hill broke his arm and leg. I picked him up and jogged the rest of the way, heading towards Shore's cabin.

\*\*\*\*\*\*\*\*\*\*\*

I dragged my father into the lake when I made it to Shore's cabin. He didn't turn when I took him underneath, he was drowning instead. I brought him back up and he smirked.

"I always wanted to know the feeling of drowning," he said.

I carried him out of the water and knocked on Shore's door, but she didn't answer.

*Fuck it.*

The door didn't have a lock, so I welcomed myself inside. Her scent lingered throughout the cabin, my father smelled it, too.

"She smells heavenly. I bet she's just as beautiful," he whispered.

I rushed him into Shore's mother's bedroom and laid him down on her bed.

"I gotta fix your arm and leg."

"Let me die, son. Just let me die. I've been dead since your mother was killed," he mumbled with his eyes closed. He grunted in pain when I snapped his leg and arm back into place.

"You told me she left."

"It was my fault she died," he replied.

I left out the cabin and sat on Shore's favorite rock. The sun was setting and the moon was beginning to rise. My wounds were healed but the pain was still there. I had two choices: let my father live or let him die.

*Yo, where the hell is Shore at?* I thought.

# Shore

Pearl took us to the deserted beach where the haunted looking mansion sat. Most of the windows were boarded up and the outside of the house looked like it was caught on fire. We stepped off the bus with all of our shopping bags and Reef was carrying the mirror, not wanting to share with everyone else. The front door opened, and it was Giva.

"We got you a few things, Mother," Rain said, walking up the steps to the house. Giva hugged me when I stepped into the foyer.

"Welcome home. We were expecting you and your mother to join us after a while, but you have a bedroom here," she said.

"I want to wait for her at the cabin."

"Where did she go?" she asked.

"To get help for her addiction."

"Okay, well, Jewel is down the hall in the pool room. Come upstairs when you're finished talking to her," she said. Giva took the bags out of my hands and took them to my room. Rain escorted me to the pool room. The inside didn't look as bad as it did on the outside. Instead, it was filled with plants and water fountains. It felt more like a forest than a house. Rain knocked on the double wooden doors.

"Comeeee innnnnn!" Jewel sang.

Rain opened the door and Jewel was in a swimming pool with fish. Two male fairies were in the pool with her. One was kissing on her neck and the other was feeding her tomatoes.

"My beautiful niece. Welcome home. Come and join me," Jewel said. She gestured for the men to leave. Their bodies almost resembled Zambezi's except for the razor-sharp gold fins and their hair didn't change. I covered my eyes when they both walked past me with their dicks swinging.

"I'll be upstairs," Rain said, closing the door behind her.

"How was your outing?" she asked.

"It was fun," I said while looking around.

The pool room was like a treasure chest; there was gold, diamonds and gems everywhere.

"Take whatever you want," she said.

"I'm fine."

"Come in. I want to see your tail," she said.

I undressed and joined Jewel in the pool.

"You have a sparkling tail like your mother's, more beautiful of course but don't tell her I told you," she smiled. The fish inside the pool swam around me, some were even eating the germs off my scales.

"Those are red garras. They clean your scales, making them shiny and even glow at night. Once a month, you will soak in a pool with them," she said. Jewel swam to the end of the pool and grabbed a gold pitcher, which resembled the golden genie lamp in *Aladdin*. She poured the wine into a small glass then swam back to me.

"Sea wine?"

"Well, of course. We don't drink what your mother drinks. Human alcohol temporarily disables our gift," she said.

"Is that why my mother drinks? So, she won't need the water?"

"Bingo," Jewel said.

"Why would my mother do that?"

"Guilt. I think she blames herself for the death of one of our reef's sisters. Me and your mother were born from the same egg at the bottom of the sea but the others who were born from different eggs, are what we call reef sisters. The same as you and Rain," she said.

"What happened to her? How did she die?"

"She was killed by some type of creature and Oceana left the waters right after it happened.

The Mediterranean Sea was red with our sister's blood for three days," she replied.

"What was her name?"

"Harbor. Open your locket," Jewel said.

"It won't open."

"Yes, it will. Tell it to open," she replied.

"Just hold it and tell it to open?"

"Your mother used to talk to it, maybe you can, too," Jewel said.

"Open," I said into the locket.

"No, in our language, before we learned how to speak English. Don't stress yourself, your mother didn't tell you anything," she said.

"*Tiya juti casti ju rue?*"

I whispered the words I heard in my dreams.

The locket opened, and bloody water dripped from inside. There were images inside a mirror. A woman with the same complexion as Zambezi was in the water with my mother. She handed my mother a baby with a wild and curly mane of jet-black hair. When I looked up from the locket, I was no longer in the pool with Jewel. I was near a small island somewhere in the sea. They couldn't see me, but I was right there with them.

"He's so beautiful," my mother said to the woman.

"I named him Zambezi. I have to hurry back before Caspian finishes hunting. I'm not supposed to be near the reef," the woman said.

"I understand, you're his mate now. You don't need to be here with us. Take this necklace, it's a gift for the baby since we couldn't be there when you gave birth. In case we never see each other again, he'll be protected," my mother replied. The woman wiped a tear away and it seemed like they were saying their final goodbye.

"What are you going to name her?" the woman asked my mother. She touched my mother's stomach and that's when I noticed she was pregnant—with me.

"I don't know yet," my mother smiled.

"Well, I hope she and Zambezi find each other in case we never see each other again. I know she'll have a good spirit since she comes from you. They can be best friends, maybe even soul mates. So together our blood can flow through their offspring," she said.

"Be safe, Harbor. We're reef sisters for eternity," my mother said. Harbor wrapped Zambezi against her body before she disappeared underneath the water. Then the images faded away and my surroundings changed. I was back in the pool with Jewel.

"What did you see?" Jewel asked.

"Harbor, Zambezi's mother."

"Zambezi's father blamed your mother for his mate's death. Shortly afterwards, your mother disappeared. No matter where she goes, we go and make a home. I'm not the real goddess, your mother is. If she doesn't return, you will have to take her place. The waters need a real queen," Jewel said.

"But they respect you."

"Just because she's my sister but I can't open the locket. I spent years saying the same words you just chanted, and it didn't open for me," Jewel replied.

"Where do we come from?"

"We were born when the waters were born. So, we come from the earth. We have gods and rulers who were here before human mankind. There is a king in the sky that shoots through the clouds like a fallen star. Then you have people whose spirits are connected to cats. There are more immortals than we think, we're just starting to blend well with humans," Jewel said. I took a sip of wine and the taste wasn't as bad as the last time.

"Why do me and Zambezi really have the same symbol?"

"It was your mother's doing before she lost her mind. But don't tell him I didn't curse him, so he can protect you. I want to ruffle his feathers for a while. Zambezi thinks we're not trustworthy because of his father but help him find his way. Harbor and Oceana would have wanted that," she said. Jewel stepped out of the pool after her tail disappeared.

"I hate to say this, but I have given up on my sister. My faith is with you now. Oceana died the moment she lost her memory," Jewel said, grabbing her robe off a chair.

"What about my father?"

"That you will have to ask Oceana when she wakes from the dead," Jewel stated before leaving me inside the pool. I finished the rest of the wine before getting out of the pool to go upstairs. There was giggling and laughter coming from the end of the hall. I knocked on the door and Lake opened it. The room was big enough to be a library. There were mirrors everywhere and vanity sets.

"This is our dressing room," Lake said.

"This is soooo Hollywood," I beamed.

"Make it rain, fish sticks!" Reef yelled out while twerking on a table without any clothes on. Rain threw money at her and the others followed.

"It's your turn, Shore. Show us what you're working with," Darya said.

"Listen, I sat in the house all my life watching videos on the internet. I can out dance all of you!" I slurred. I was a little drunk. It snuck up on me out of nowhere.

"Go ahead," they said.


Someone turned the radio on and a rap song was on. They cheered me on when I popped my butt to the beat. The fairies were throwing money and jewelry on the table.

"Who needs a mate when we can party together every night, drink wine, spend money and fuck whoever we want to? This is the life!" Reef shouted. We all were dancing and passing the wine bottle. After the song went off, I almost fell off the table, but someone caught me.

"Damn, she's hammered. Poor thing never had a drink in her life until today. Here, smoke this," Rain said. She stuffed some kind of stringy grass inside a snail shell and placed a match against it.

"Inhale this," she said.

My throat felt like it was swelling, and my chest burned. They burst into laughter.

"What is that?"

"Sea kelp soaked in squid ink. It's the best feeling in the world," Rain said.

"I don't think we're going anywhere tonight," Darya said, inhaling the sea kelp.

The room was spinning, and I heard echoes in my head. I placed my finger in my ear and wiggled it around because the noise was too loud.

"STOPPPP!" I screamed, and the windows inside the room shattered and so did all the mirrors.

"She ruined our mirrors," someone said.

"You ugly anyway," Reef joked.

They started arguing, complaining about the shattered mirrors. I left the room, looking for a way to leave.

"Wait, Shore! Where are you going?" Rain ran after me.

"Home!" I shouted then tumbled down the stairs. I hit my head on the floor.

"Holy shit!" Rain ran down the stairs and the girls followed suit.

"I think we overdid it. I forgot she was a couch potato," Reef said. She placed her ear against my chest to see if I was still alive and I mushed her into the wall.

"Take me to Zambeziiiiiiiii. I want him to hold me and touch me with his tongue. Do you all know he has a vibrating tongue? I came soooooo hard and for a very longggg time!" my words slurred.

"Wait a minute! Did she say his tongue vibrates?" Reef jumped up.

"Doesn't Zambezi have a little brother?" Lake asked.

"I get him first! I'm the most mature one here," Rain said.

"I'm older than you!" Lake yelled at her.

"But I make sure we're safe when we all go out and I fight people who start shit with us, so therefore I get the baby vibrator," Rain said.

"That's not fair at all. You all take advantage of the ones who don't talk much," Darya said.

"According to the humans, closed mouths don't get fed. Now, this is how it goes. Rain can try him out first then me. Y'all figure out your turns from there," Reef said.

"Why can't we just have Zambezi?" someone said.

"We don't share mates, pickle head," Lake replied.

"What did y'all do to me?" I groaned; my head was throbbing. Thinking about Zambezi made me aroused. My nipples ached and I was beginning to sweat.

"You didn't tell her that was a stimulant, too? Do you do anything right?" Lake asked Reef.

"Oops, I'm sorry, Shore. I forgot," Reef said.

I almost fell again when I stood up, but I grabbed ahold of the rail.

"Let's swim Shore home," Rain said.

"Then after we're done, we can see what humans are out on the water in their boats, so we can scare them," Reef said.

"That is so whack," Lake said.

I headed towards the door because their bickering was giving me a headache. The breeze from the waves immediately soothed me after I stepped outside. My vision was blurry, and my legs were weak, but I had to get to Zambezi. My reef sisters followed me into the water on the beach. They lured me further out into the deep end before diving under. Rain and Reef helped guide me through the ocean. My eyelids grew heavy and I fell asleep.

# Zambezi

I t was one o'clock in the morning and Shore still wasn't home. I wanted to go find her, but I couldn't chance Adwoa coming to take my father. I'd been on the rock for hours, waiting for Shore. I was pissed off and my mind started wandering.

*What if she's on a date? Hell no, Shore is too shy for that. But then again, she was hanging with water fairies. They are promiscuous and seek a lot of attention. Naw, fuck that, I'll have to tie her to me. Whoa! Bro, you trippin.' Man up! This ain't your style...*

I gave up and slid off the rock. While I was heading towards the cabin, the waves in the lake were picking up. I saw four water fairy tails sticking out of the water. Two of them stepped out of the water, dragging one by her arms while her head was slumped over. I noticed it was

Shore when I got closer. I rushed to her and pulled her away from them. Shore burst out laughing when I picked her up.

"You're so big and strong," Shore said.

She was naked and aroused. Shore licked my ear while whispering to me.

"I want to sit on your face while you fuck my hole with your tongue," she said. Her friends must've heard her because they were snickering. They followed me into the cabin and I laid Shore on her bed. She pulled me towards her and slipped her tongue into my mouth.

"Y'all think this is funny, huh? Why are y'all in here?"

"Because we want to know where your brother is. Just tell me where and I'll be out of your hair," Rain said.

"And hurry up with it. Shore isn't the only one aroused," Reef said.

"I agree, and I'm Lake by the way," she said.

"Y'all are not using my baby brother for that bullshit!"

"We'll take good care of him at our mansion," Lake said.

Shore was pulling me on top of her, wrapping her legs around me. When she gently bit my neck, I wanted to say, "fuck it" and ram my dick into her.

"Ohh, she's wild," Reef said.

"So, y'all just gonna stand there and watch?"

"Aren't you going to put your magical tongue on her?" Lake asked.

I pulled away from Shore to escort her friends out. They were giggling and laughing, one of them even pinched me and broke skin on the sly.

"Did one of you just pinch me?"

Water fairies were like misbehaved kids and if Shore had their behavior, I wouldn't be able to deal with it. She was different and that was what drew me into her. In other words, she was mature.

"Would you tell me where your brother is if I tell you who did it?" Reef asked.

"I hate all of y'all with a fucking passion and I just hope one day a shark eats all of you. And you look too old for my baby brother," I said, talking to Lake. They gasped, and Lake burst into tears.

"Where's the mirror? I need to find one? Do I look old? Oh, my heavens! Quick, find me a mirror," Lake said.

"Why would you tell her that?" Reef yelled at me. Her teeth changed, and her nails grew out into sharp hooks.

"I'm gonna scratch your eyes out!" Reef hissed.

They backed away when the bones in my body shifted. My arms swelled while expanding outwards. The flesh on my body was shedding and tearing, making room for my growth. My back twisted and cracked as my spine grew. The water fairies backed away from me when I stood over them with menacing eyes and a mouth big enough to swallow a boat. The paws of my dragon slammed against the ground and the cabin shook.

My dragon opened its mouth, shooting out a gust of water. Shore's friends went sailing across the lake. They stuck their heads out of the water and gave me the finger.

"We're not scared of you! I'm going to make a reptile-skin bra out of you while you're sleeping! This isn't over, bitch!" Reef screamed. I shrank back into my human form and grabbed a canoe next to Shore's cabin. They screamed and cursed me out when I strong-armed the canoe across the lake.

"You almost hit my sister with it!" Rain said.

"Go the fuck home before I turn again and eat y'all dumb asses!"

"We're going to find another mate for Shore!" Lake said.

"Take your old ass to bed before you end up in my fish market on ice!"

That pissed them off because one of them threw a fish at me. They were gone by the time I made it back inside the cabin. Shore was on the floor sleeping. Her bed was too small for the both of us, so I laid her down then left out of her room to check up on my father. He was still asleep.

*Now what am I going to do? If I go back home, I might have to kill Adwoa. Maybe Shore would let us crash here and I could pay her until I find a home outside of Oland. All I need is a week.*

I went back inside Shore's room and leaned against the wall next to her bed. Sleep was the last thing on my mind. Adwoa had to die but I needed a way to do it without Bay finding out, but I couldn't take chances on that. Shore turned in her sleep, her head hanging over the bed and her hair sprawled out over the floor. When I picked her head back up, she opened her eyes and smiled at me.

"We belong together. Our mothers wanted this for us and we must do it for them because all we have left of them is us," she said. Shore reached out and touched my face.

"I'll slit your throat if you hurt me," she said. She laid back down and fell back to sleep.

*These bipolar water fairies are going to be the death of me.*

## Eight hours later...

"Zambezi wake up!"

Shore was kneeling in front of me when I opened my eyes. Her face was refreshed, and she was wearing a bathing suit cover-up. Her scent gave me a morning erection. I looked at my watch and it was close to nine thirty.

"Who is that man in my mother's room?" she asked.

"My father."

When I stretched out my legs, Shore turned her head because my dick was standing tall, almost ripping the crotch of my shorts, wanting to break free. I grabbed her hand and placed it on my erection.

"You talked all that shit this morning. If you were sober, I would've definitely had spread your legs."

"I had a wild night at the fairy's mansion. Did you come get me?"

"Naw, they brought you here. If they tell you I did something to them, don't believe it," I chuckled.

"What did you do to them?" she laughed.

"Pissed them off."

She pulled her hand away from me and when she stood up, her scent crept into my nostrils, making the monster in me grunt. A deep rattling sound with a low growl came from inside me. I wanted Shore. It seemed like she was getting more beautiful by the day and her plump ass was big enough for my monster hands to grip while pounding the pink and wet flesh between her mound. I had to feel her, it didn't even matter if I couldn't enter her at that moment. She fell onto my lap when I pulled her towards me. Her hot center was pressed against my erection. She wrapped her arms around me and licked my lips. I squeezed her ass, and she was leaking on my shorts. I released myself, pressing the head of my shaft against her center but careful not to hurt her. Her breasts swelled, and her nipples puckered out.

"Take this off."

Shore took off her cover-up and her soft cantaloupe-sized breasts bounced with each movement of her arms. I placed them inside my mouth, sucking on her star-shaped nipples. Her nails scratched at my scalp while holding my head against her chest, slowly moving her hips back and forth. The veins in my dick swelled against Shore's clit. Her essence flooded my dick. Her moans were soft, passionate and intoxicating. Hearing her moan was enough to make me bust. Her pussy lips gripped my dick while gliding across the tip. My nails were buried deeply into the flesh of her buttocks, while I bit her neck. She pressed her hands against the wall, to keep her steady while grinding on my girth. Shore was practically giving me a lap dance. My dick swelled between her pussy lips. I tasted my own blood from biting my bottom lip.

"Fuck, beautiful," I gritted.

Shore's legs trembled, and her eyes rolled upwards while her nails dug into my chest. She was squirting, and I wanted to taste her. I picked Shore up and placed her above head. Her knees were pressed onto my shoulders and her pussy was creaming. A gruntling sound came from my dragon when she dripped on my tongue, her sticky-like essence hitting the back of my throat.

Shore grabbed the window sill to keep her balance while I kissed her wet lips. Her body jerked when my tongue vibrated against her clit. She rode my face, taking in the pleasure and controlling her body. Unlike the first time, Shore was more comfortable. She didn't tell me to stop, she wanted more. Her legs squeezed my head when I sucked on her tight hole. My dick was still covered in her essence, throbbing and jerking from the pressure of arousal. My shaft was aching, causing cramping in my pelvic area. I grabbed my piece, jerking it off to ease the pressure. The harder I stroked the more I slurped on Shore's pussy. She pressed my face into her while she cried out my name. My dick exploded like a champagne bottle, spilling over onto the floor. I pulled Shore off my shoulders and sat her on my lap. She laid against my chest and I rubbed her back. She hummed a sweet melody and it was relaxing. The stress I was dealing with was pulling away from me. I didn't want her to stop.

"I needed this."

"I know," she replied.

"How do you know my mother? You said something about her when you came home."

"I saw images of them. Our mothers were reef sisters. The necklace you wear was a gift from my mother. I didn't see much but from what I could make out your necklace protects you. This locket must've showed me the last time my mother wore it because blood was inside when I opened it. Something bad happened that day when we lost our mothers. We're going to find out the truth," she replied.

"What does she look like? My father never told me my mother was a water fairy. I thought she was a serpent."

"She was beautiful with the same skin tone you have," she said.

"What was her name?"

"Harbor. She looked very young, too, like an eighteen-year-old. Seems like my mother really cared for her but your father didn't want her to be with her kind anymore," Shore said.

"Get up real quick."

Shore moved away from me, so I could fix myself. I smelled like sex and needed a shower, but it didn't stop me from barging into the bedroom my father was lying in.

"Get up!" I shouted.

Shore ran into the bedroom and stood in front of me.

"He's sick!" she shouted.

"Fuck him. Fathers don't lie to their offspring. I'm just finding out my mother was killed. He promised since I was a little boy he was going to find her or at least help me, and come to find out she's dead. That son-of-a-bitch needs to die."

"He's your father!" she said.

"So, what, you're siding with him?"

"No, but you only have one parent alive!" she shouted.

My father winced when he sat up in the bed and Shore helped him up.

"I have some ingredients left over from Giva. I can make you some soup," Shore told him.

"Why are you trying to feed him?"

"This isn't you, Zambezi. I know you're angry, but something happened to your father for him to be like this. Whatever it is can be fixed, and plus, everyone deserves a second chance," she said. Shore left out of the room and my father smirked.

"She's got a lot of courage. I never wanted my sons to get wrapped up in those fairies. You'll fall in love, but they'll choose their reef sisters over their mate. Their bond is unbreakable so if you love one, you have to accept the rest. I wish I knew that before your mother was killed. If I hadn't forbidden her from seeing her sisters, she wouldn't have snuck out when the waters weren't safe. She was depressed from that and it changed our love," he said.

"What is Adwoa? She disguises herself as a water fairy, but I saw the real her when she attacked me yesterday."

"I don't know what she is but whatever it is weakened me. Something else is in my head," he replied.

"Get some rest. I'll be back, I have to get some clothes for us."

He placed his hand on my shoulder. "If you let me die, I will still love you." I pulled away from him and left out of the room. Shore was sitting at the table with fresh herbs and spices. She was humming while chopping up seaweed.

"If it's okay with you, we might have to crash here for a week. I'll find a place by then, but it won't be in Oland. When I come back, I'm going to start repairing the house."

"I enjoy the company. I'll keep an eye out for your father while you're gone," she smiled.

"Appreciate you."

I grabbed my shoes then headed out of the cabin.

**\*\*\*\*\*\*\*\*\***

The door to my father's cabin was wide-open when I approached the house. The scent of Adwoa's candle was gone and the coldness that was once there was replaced by warmth. I went into Bay's bedroom and he wasn't in there.

*He's gotta be at the market.*

I rushed to my father's bedroom to grab his clothes. After I left, I went into my cabin and it was destroyed on the inside.

"What the fuck!" I dropped my father's clothes in disbelief. Despite wanting to move away, it was the first thing I'd built on my own. I heard a crashing noise coming from my bedroom. Before I turned, I sniffed the air to make sure it wasn't a human. The fragrance of the perfume was familiar. When I went inside my bedroom, Laguna was lying on my bed naked and crying.

"Yo, get the fuck out!"

She sat up and wiped her eyes.

"Where were you?" she asked.

"I'm not your concern."

"I know you were at that cabin with Shore. Adwoa told me all about it when I saw her this morning. You left me for her? What does she have, huh? She's poor!" Laguna said.

"But those Chanel pumps in my living room are from the flea market and I still fucked you, so maybe I don't care about that."

"I'm not letting you go so easily. We shared something very special," she said.

"What did we do besides go to clubs and have sex? We never had a real conversation. Shore knows more shit about me in less than a week. We're over with."

"Adwoa told me you'd say that," she said.

"Y'all friends or something?"

"She's been teaching me her religion. Every night around midnight, most of the people gather in the woods to listen to her speak," Laguna said.

"What kind of religion is this?"

"To gain wealth, live longer and stay beautiful. I'm here to surrender to you and be yours for eternity," she said.

"Adwoa is forming a cult. What do you have to do to gain these things?"

"I'll tell you if let me in," she said.

Laguna's eyes turned blue and her teeth were sharper than usual.

"This can't be."

Laguna walked over to me and grabbed my dick through my shorts.

"Let me be yours and I'll tell you everything," she said. I pushed Laguna away from me and her eyes turned black.

"Bro, you in here?" Bay called out.

"I'm in the room!" I shouted over my shoulder.

When I turned back around, Laguna was climbing out of the window. Shit was getting weirder every day.

"What happened?" Bay asked.

"Laguna did this. You noticed anything strange in the town?"

"I just came from the market. Nobody was there. The town was empty. Did you see my mother? She didn't come home last night, and Father is gone, too," he said.

"The markets were empty?"

"It's like a ghost town," he replied.

"Bro tell me you'll never lie to me because the way things are going, I can't trust anyone right now. How is the town a ghost town when it was crowded just yesterday?"

"I don't know. I went there and opened the market, but nobody showed up. I'm not saying everybody actually left but it wasn't normal. I only saw the elderly humans and there were only a few of them," Bay said. I was listening to his thoughts while he was talking in case he stumbled over his words.

"You can't stay here anymore. Your mother lost her fuckin' mind last night. I don't know what she did, but Father is dying because of her. You said yourself we need to live somewhere else."

"You don't think it's Shore? Everything was fine until she showed up," he said.

"They fear her for a reason but she's good. But on the real, I'm on whatever side she's on. So, if she's bad for this town, I'm going to protect her. Besides, you can help me fix up her cabin. Grab your things and a tent or something. We gotta camp out until I find us a spot."

"Aight," Bay said. He wasn't feeling what I told him to do but he didn't have a choice. Bay left out of my cabin to go next door for his things. I was putting a lot of pressure on Shore by moving my father and brother in, so I owed her a lot. Once I finished grabbing everything I needed, I headed back out to return to Shore's cabin.

# Adwoa

**A week later...**

"Did you find her?"

"No, Adwoa. Oceana left and went into the city. I followed her trail but lost her. I've been looking for her for a week and nothing," Lesidi said.

"You've been gone all this time and you bring me back nothing? I thought she was dead! You told me you killed her and her offspring twenty years ago. Oceana and her daughter alive will ruin this whole clan especially if they heal Caspian. You had one fucking job!" I yelled. The old abandoned ship creaked from my anger. I slammed a table into the wall and Lesidi ducked from the fallen wood.

"My children come!" I shouted.

The people from the town of Oland came into the ship and kneeled before me. They were my children. During the day we were a regular small town. We owned stores, markets, danced and sang but by nightfall we gave our spirits to Elonora, a demon of the sea. She saved us from the ships and gave us immortality. The day I died was the day I was reborn. Back home in my village, we worshipped the goddess of the waters. We believed she was the healer of sickness and could help us find a way home if we got lost in the sea. But what we thought was true, was only true for Oceana's kind. She was only a goddess to her people. We worshipped her, and she failed us.

In front of me were over one hundred people. I did what Elonora did for me and gave them a better life. They weren't falling sick or aging. Oland was special to me. After the original settlers passed on, it was left to us. I lit the candle next to my chair. It was of Caspian's blood that I drained from him while he slept. Burning a candle of a sea dragon's blood kept them immortal.

"Caspian is weak now. His blood won't cure you anymore. There are only two candles left. Zambezi has the same blood type and he's young. We can use him for many, many years to stay immortal. We cannot have his blood until he claims one of us as his. If he falls in love with Shore, she'll have him, and his heart will be guarded. The only way to keep that from happening is to kill her! We have one month before we start aging and feeling sick again," I said.

"Why can't we use Bay's blood?" his girlfriend, Ara, asked.

"He's not mature. His blood won't heal us, but I want you to bring him to me before they feed him lies and ruin him," I replied.

"When can we return back to our homes?" Katana, Laguna's mother, asked.

"After Shore is dead. Zambezi knows about the candles now, so we will stay here until the problem is fixed. Now, you all are dismissed!" They left from the ship and I blew out the candle to save its wax. With the candle out, I felt somewhat mortal. Cold tears fell from my eyes thinking about the chains that were once around my ankles. I wanted revenge for the family I lost even though I could no longer remember their names or their faces. Images flashed before my eyes of me watching many people drown underneath a ship.

*The bottom of the ship was flooding. Screams pained my ears and the pregnant woman named Lesidi was clutching her stomach because of her baby. We were chained and couldn't escape. The voice I'd been hearing told me it was okay to relax. She promised me that I would live again after I died.*

*"Oceana, please do something now. The rest of the people are drowning."*

*"I will give them life but it's you I want. Relax and let the water take you," the voice said inside my head.*

*I did what Oceana told me to do and let the bottom of the ship fill with water. Lesidi grabbed a hold of my hand and squeezed. She jerked, and I heard muffled screams underneath from people dying. Water filled my lungs, suffocating me. The ship crashed, causing the water to spill out. I choked up water when it cleared, but I was still drowning. A figure appeared in front of me and it was a woman. Her skin was gray, and her hair was white. One of her eyes was white, too, and the other was black. Her nails were bloody, and I could see the ribs in her skin. She kneeled beside me and looked into my eyes. I thought I'd died, and death was staring at me. Her teeth were sharp and overlapping one another. She placed her lips against mine and sucked the water out of my body.*

*"Oceana?"*

*I'd heard stories about Oceana being the most beautiful creature in the waters. The woman next to me looked like the demons my family told me about. The thing transformed into a beautiful fair-skinned woman with orange wavy hair.*

*"You're strong and was the only one willing to sacrifice your life to the waters. Because you deeply worship Oceana, I will give you a gift from myself. You will be my vessel and live for eternity," she said. Lesidi was coughing and choking beside me; she was the only other one alive.*

*"Help her," I strained.*

*"Do you accept this gift, Adwoa? You have to accept it before I can give it to you. If you don't, the water will fill your lungs again. Do you accept to worship me and do what you must for our kingdom?" she asked.*

*"YES!"*

*She healed Lesidi then she disappeared.*

*"What did you do, Adwoa? What did you do? That was a sea demon! You accepted her deal and now we'll be dead like her forever. We should've followed fate and died. I heard her voice, too, but I ignored her. Oceana is a myth, but the sea demon is real. She tricked you! Now we will suffer. You'll have to live for hundreds of years and then our body will look like hers," Lesidi said.*

*"Lies you speak!"*

*"I'm not lying to you, Adwoa. Sea demons haunt the water, looking for worshippers. If you come into the waters and ask for Oceana, she'll come to you instead, pretending to be her and trick you," she said.*

*"I won't hurt anyone."*

*"Now I have to obey you because you asked her to save me," she said...*

I couldn't hear Elonora anymore, but I could feel her, and I did everything she wanted. Soon, I'd have thousands believing in her—us. Once we grew, we'd be able to take over the land and the waters. It was our world.

# Sabrina

"How much do I owe you?"

"It's ten dollars and nineteen cents," the cashier said. I placed the twenty-dollar bill on the counter and he put the small bottle of whiskey inside the brown paper bag. After he gave me the change back, I walked out the liquor store. A homeless man was sitting in front of the liquor store with a can, asking for spare change. I gave him two dollars and he thanked me. My motel room was around the corner. I was in the trenches of North East D.C., three hours away from Oland in driving distance. With nowhere else to go, I was practically homeless with only twenty dollars left to my name. I gave Shore most of the money I had secretly saved over the years because I eventually knew I had to leave her. Lying to my daughter was the hardest thing I had to do, but she deserved better. She didn't need me anymore. I kicked off my shoes and got comfortable on the full-size bed, pushing the other bottles onto the floor. In less than two minutes, the bottle of whiskey was gone. Falling back onto the bed, I stared at the ceiling fan. The liquor consumed me, relieving me from the past. I closed my eyes when the feeling of drowsiness settled in...

*I watched Harbor swim away with her baby tied around her with sea grass. She was returning home to her mate for good. She only came to say goodbye forever. The sun was setting, and the clouds were getting darker. Her tail glowed as the rest of her blended in with the water. Once she was out of sight, I opened my locket to keep an eye on her. My locket showed me visions of the waters like lakes, rivers, ponds, the ocean and sea, so no matter where I went, they were still connected to me. A group of big gray fish surrounded Harbor. Looking closer into the mirror inside the locket, they had red and black eyes with human-like faces. Harbor placed the necklace around her baby's neck, so it could protect him. I swam as fast as I could, diving deeper into the ocean. A loud whistle rang through my gills to alert my reef sisters of Harbor. The sharks in the water swam underneath me to attack. The gray fish creatures were biting Harbor when I approached them. A strong sound wave rippled through the waters, slicing through their flesh. More of them came, there were many. I grabbed Harbor and one of them took her baby. My reef sisters came, and the once blue ocean was filled with blood. Pearl bit a chuck of flesh off the creature's neck that took Harbor's baby and rescued him. I swam to the surface and Harbor's neck was sliced in half. Her head fell off into the water while holding her lifeless body. Something from underneath tore gashes into my tail before pulling me under. Many of them surrounded me. The baby inside of my womb was slowing me down. I couldn't fight any longer, so I swam away with them chasing behind me. The sharks ate some of them, but more were still coming. We were outnumbered. A heavy rock fell onto my head while I was trying to escape. The gray creatures tackled my body, sharp teeth tore at my flesh and my locket was snatched away from me while protecting my stomach. A gigantic monster with a big mouth blew us through the ocean—it was a sea dragon. After I passed out from the impact, I woke up on a shore, naked and battered with memory loss.*

I gasped when I woke up with my stomach in knots. Vomit came up in my throat and I ran into the bathroom, throwing up all the liquor inside my body. After I was finished, I washed my face. When I looked into the mirror above the sink, the reflection was of what I used to be in the waters. My jet-black hair with gold highlights draped down my breasts, shielding them.

"What did you do to yourself, Oceana?"

The reflection disappeared, and I saw the dark circles around my eyes and matted hair. The clothes I wore I had on for a week and they were soaked with sweat. The gray creatures were still out there, and I had to get rid of them, once and for all. While taking a shower, I hummed the song I used to sing to my reef sisters. Before I returned back to the waters, I had to get rid of the poison in my body, so I could swim again. Once I was finished with the shower, I grabbed a towel and went into the bedroom. Next to the telephone on the nightstand was a pamphlet for alcoholics. I had to do what I promised Shore in the letter. It was the only way Shore and the waters could stay safe.

"You don't need that, Oceana. I'll help you," a voice said from behind me. I dropped the pamphlet. My nerves were all over the place.

"Damn it, Giva. My nerves are bad. How did you get in here?"

"I came out of the sink. You do remember we can turn our bodies into water," she said.

"Where is Jewel?"

"She's home. Jewel doesn't know I am here. She's very upset with you and she doesn't want me to talk to you, but I can't stay away. Seeing you like this crushes me. Plus, your daughter needs you. I'm going to help you get better. We can learn how to swim again but you cannot go to that place and get clean. You might turn into something that'll show the humans what we are," Giva said. I sat on the bed and she placed her hand on my shoulder.

"I'll be back and forth here but you can do this, Oceana. The queen must return," Giva said.

"I will return, I promise I will."

*I must return. I can't let Shore take on my responsibilities of the waters when she's never been exposed to them until now.*

# Shore

Zambezi was waiting on customers inside his market while I was in the back putting ice on the fish and shrimp. We'd been together for a week and with his brother and father living with me, we were like family. Me and Bay took turns going with Zambezi to his market in the city because someone had to stay back with Caspian. Zambezi came into the freezer room wearing rubber gloves and rubber boots. He wiped the sweat off his forehead with his forearm. The market was busy, and it was just us, but the crowd was dying down. He grabbed four big pails of lobsters and I followed him to the front with a tray of rainbow trout.

"What's up, beautiful," a voice said from behind me. It was Nerida again. He was wearing khaki shorts and a polo shirt with a pair of casual shoes.

"Oh hey. Do you want shrimp again?"

"Naw, I came here for oysters this time. Happy to know you remember me," he said.

"My memory is pretty decent. But the oysters are over here."

Nerida followed me to the oyster counter. He grabbed the metal scoop and a bag. After he placed the oysters in the bag, I took them to the front counter to weigh them.

"Sixty dollars," I told him.

"Can I take you out tonight?" he asked while going inside his pocket.

"Naw, bruh. She good," Zambezi said from behind me. Nerida was embarrassed but he hid it well.

"Oh, my bad, slim. I didn't know that was you," he said, grabbing the oysters off the counter.

"Have a nice day," I smiled.

"The offer still stands to dine at my family's restaurant. You can bring anyone you want, it's on me," Nerida said on his way out the market.

"You're such a blocker," I teased.

"I'm gonna remember that the next time you trash the phone numbers the women slide to me," he said.

"Don't get full of yourself. I was looking out for you."

"I was looking out for you, too. Dude was a straight lame. You didn't see the clear polish on his nails? He's definitely a fairy," he said.

"He's not gay."

"Are rainbow fish colorful?" he chuckled.


**An hour later...**


I locked the doors and mopped the floors after the market closed. While I was cleaning, Zambezi was counting the money. It amazed me how much money he made from selling seafood, but it was very popular, especially during the summer. He took the mop away from me and handed me a stack of money.

"We don't have to go straight back to Oland after this. We can chill if you want. Plus, I want to show you something," he said.

"I smell like seafood and my clothes are dirty."

"I already brought you something. There is a small shower in the back," he said. I took off my clothes in front of him while backing away.

"You coming?" I asked.

"Hell yeah."

We went into the small bathroom and it was too short for Zambezi because his head almost touched the ceiling. He almost elbowed me when he took off his shirt.

"Did you get taller or something?"

"Naw, this shit is just for average-sized humans," he replied.

He stepped into the shower with me and he was taller than the shower head. Zambezi was getting frustrated and I couldn't stop laughing because he was ducking under the shower head to get wet.

"Move! I can't get to the water!"

"Hold on, damn. My knees starting to hurt," he complained.

"Crybaby."

I helped Zambezi wash his back, so I could have my turn. After he rinsed off, he helped me. My head rested against his chest while he washed my hair. He kissed my neck while washing my breasts. Everything he did to my body was amazing. Even though I was still a virgin, Zambezi showed me ways to pleasure him. He playfully nibbled on my ear while washing between my legs. His sharp canines scraped against my skin, tickling me. Zambezi's dick was pressed against my backside. Afterwards, he handed me a towel once we were finished.

"I'll get your clothes. I'll be right back," he said. He grabbed a towel and wrapped it around his waist then left out of the bathroom. I sat on the toilet seat to dry off and something underneath the sink caught my eye; it was a woman's thong. We hadn't established what we were to each other yet, but it angered me. I'd watched a few women throw themselves at Zambezi and he'd just smirk at them. He came back into the bathroom minutes later, dressed in ripped shorts and a basketball jersey with a pair of tennis shoes I hadn't seen before. He also had two bags in his hand from Saks.

"Me and Bay went to the mall yesterday and I got you a few things. I hope I did good because I never shopped for a woman," he said. But I was fighting to keep my cool. Fish scales covered my legs and the shape of my nails changed into long hooks.

"I did something?" he asked.

"Look under the sink!"

Zambezi sat the bags on the floor and bent over to look underneath the sink. He used his shoe to pull the thong out.

"Yo, I don't know who those belong to. You think I'm going to mess around with a customer while you're here? Matter of fact, I wouldn't do that here at all. What kind of dude do you mistake me for?" he asked. I don't know where the anger came from but I couldn't hold it in any longer. When I screamed, it was a high-pitched screech loud enough to make someone deaf. The mirror on the wall cracked and the toilet exploded. Zambezi covered my mouth and pressed me against the wall.

"Stop before you fuck up the market!" he yelled. I scratched his arm and he wrestled me onto the floor.

*Stop, Shore! Just stop!*

I so badly wanted to stop but something came over me. I was trapped inside of a body that wasn't listening to me. I couldn't control myself. I got away from Zambezi and ran into the shower, balling up in the corner, afraid.

*Shore, he's not trying to hurt you! Stop acting like this!*

"I'll let you calm down while I check up on the rest of my store," he said before leaving out of the bathroom. I noticed my body was covered in silver scales and I had fins as feet instead of a tail. It was the first time seeing my body change that way. Zambezi came back and leaned against the doorway of the bathroom.

"A few windows cracked but it's nothing I can't fix. Mind telling me what that was about?"

"Why do I look like this?"

"Your kind is bipolar and I'm not being a jack-ass. I don't think y'all can control it. I could be wrong but maybe you do this when feeling threatened; this might be your bad side. Don't trip, I have that side, too. I just don't scream," he joked and just like that, I was back to normal. Zambezi took my outfit out the bag and handed me a shoe box.

"You got me Red Bottoms?"

"Yeah, I think your feet would look nice in these," he said.

They were open-toe shoes with pearls on the straps. The outfit he bought was a white off-the-shoulder top with a pair of shorts.

"The girl at the store picked that out for you so it could match your shoes. What you think?" he asked.

"These are very nice. I'm so sorry. I don't know where that came from. I don't deserve these, and I'll use the money you paid me to fix your bathroom and the windows."

"My brother and father are crashing at your spot. I owe you everything; and besides, I thought it was sexy. All you need is a monster to tame that attitude and you'll be straight," he said. He handed me my things, so I could get dressed. Since my body changed, I didn't wear bras or panties because it irritated my skin. It took less time getting dressed. Afterwards, I put my hair into a ponytail. Zambezi just stood and watched me. He did that often, just observing me. But when he wasn't looking, I did the same thing.

"Feel better now?" he asked when we left the bathroom. He wrapped his arm around me and kissed my forehead. I don't think Zambezi realized how much his attitude had changed. He was still an arrogant asshole at times, but he was attentive when it came to my feelings.

He locked the back door to the market and we headed to the dock towards the boat. Zambezi told me to get on his back, so I wouldn't slip and get dirty. When I did, he carried me to his boat. It was too soon to say I loved him, but it wouldn't have been wrong if I did. Zambezi was the first and only man to come into my life and show me things. I wanted him to be the first man to enter my body because deep down inside, I knew we were meant for each other and our mothers felt it, too.

## Two and a half hours later...

"Slow down! Bruh, you fitting to fuck up my car!" Zambezi said. From the boat, we went to an area where he kept his car which wasn't far away from Oland. Because Oland didn't have real roads, you'd take a chance on messing up your car trying to drive through. Zambezi drove a black 2018 seven series BMW. I drove my mother's car a few times when she was too drunk to drive so I was familiar with driving. A few cars honked their horns at me when I cut them off on a bridge.

"Pull over!" Zambezi said.

"Be quiet, I got this."

I slowed down, and Zambezi was cursing me out under his breath. We ended up in Alexandria, Virginia. Zambezi was giving me directions and telling me when to turn.

"Stop right here," he said when we pulled up into a driveway. We were in front of a waterfront beach-style house.

"What is this?" I asked while we were getting out of the car.

"Remember I told you I was moving out of Oland? This is it, I want to show you around," he said.

"I forgot you said that."

"You can come. We'll still be close to the water and Lake Deep isn't that far from here if you swim," he said.

"Lake Deep is close to my sisters, and what about the cave we snuck off to? This seems too humanized."

"We both know Oland is going to eventually die. We can still go back but we will live here. Besides, I have to protect you, so you pretty much don't have a choice," he said.

"Your father did the same thing to your mother."

"What the fuck did you just say to me?" Zambezi asked with glowing eyes.

"Don't talk to me like that and you heard what I said! Your father isolated your mother from her sisters and it made her hate him! I don't want her fate."

"You will stay here. Now, if you want to scream or attack me, go ahead. As soon as this house is ready to be moved into, we're gone!" he said. Zambezi punched a code in on a keypad.

"Can you please just look at it?"

I followed him into the house and it was spacious with wooden floors. It was an open floor home with three bedrooms downstairs and I wondered how many were upstairs. The huge windows around the living room overlooked the water. It was a beautiful scenery, but it wasn't like Lake Deep.

"Eventually we will have to compromise because I can't be that far away from you. We have been vibing hard this past week and I'm not trying to argue. Just don't bring up my parents because that has nothing to do with you. I know you see things in your locket, but you can't live through that. This is about Shore and Zambezi, not your reef sisters or anyone else."

"I've been moving my whole life and coming into this life has given me a different outlook. Lake Deep became my home. It's not much but it's something to me. I'm not moving with you, so if we have to be away from each other, so be it," I replied.

"Say no more," he said.

Zambezi went to the front door and waited for me. I didn't even bother with seeing the rest of the house. He locked up afterwards and I got into the passenger seat of his car.

"We can grab something to eat and even a few drinks before we go home," he said.

"Okay."

**\*\*\*\*\*\*\*\*\*\***

Thirty minutes later, Zambezi took me to a Greek restaurant. It was outside seating, and also my first time eating somewhere other than fast food spots.

"I love the color of your hair," the waitress said.

"Thank you."

She sat our menus in front of us before going back inside.

"Thank you for bringing me here. This is my first date."

"Anytime," he said.

Zambezi was somewhat quiet. I looked over the menu and decided I wanted a pasta dish.

"What are you getting?"

"Steak and potatoes," he replied.

Zambezi wasn't a vegetable or fruit eater. His diet mainly consisted of meat, bloody meat.

"I think we should talk about what happened back at your beach house." Zambezi placed the menu down on the table and leaned back in his chair.

"What's up?" he asked.

"The silence between us."

"Tired from a long day," he replied.


After our food came, we ate in silence. Zambezi didn't talk to me and I gave up trying to spark conversation. My first date wasn't what I expected. I had a feeling he was done with me and the thought made me nauseous. There was something that had to be done. I knew the silence was my fault, but I wanted him to understand I couldn't just leave because it was something he wanted. Zambezi wasn't trying to hear me out, he wanted me to do what he wanted but I couldn't because Lake Deep was in my heart too.

\*\*\*\*\*\*\*\*\*\*\*

When we made it back to Lake Deep, it was almost two o'clock in the morning. Zambezi parked his car in a different place then we came back home on his boat. We made small talk, but it wasn't the same.

"Are you coming in?" I asked. He was still sitting on the boat.

"I'll be in," he said.

I took off my shoes then jumped off the boat. When I opened the door to the cabin, Bay was sitting at the table making seaweed roll-ups for his weed.

"Oh shit. I thought you and big bro was staying out," Bay said while cleaning off the table.

"How is your father?"

"Still the same. I think we should give him what he wants. He wants to die," Bay said.

I went into the bedroom to check on Caspian and he was sitting up. He still wasn't getting better, but only because he wasn't fighting. Most of the time, he was too weak to talk. I sat on the floor next to his bed and he touched my shoulder.

"I want you to put me out of my misery," he said.

"A leader to his people doesn't speak that way."

"I'm not a leader anymore, Shore. I've done a lot of things that failed my kind," he replied.

"How did Adwoa steal your blood?"

"All she needed was me to enter her body and every time I woke up afterwards, I was weak. Then once I became weak, she controlled my mind. Just kill me!" he begged.

"You will fail your sons if you give up."

I pulled the blanket over him and left out of the room.

"Where is Zambezi?" Bay asked.

"He's outside on his boat," I replied. I sat across from Bay and he slid me a blunt.

"Zam just be trippin'. I think you got to his head. Bro never talked about a female as much as he talks about you. He also used to snap a lot, too. The smallest thing would have him ready to bite your head off. He's been cool lately," Bay said.

Zambezi came into the cabin seconds later. He had blood dripping from his mouth. He was naked with a gold shield covering his private area. His wild mane covered his face but through the hair, I saw glowing green eyes. They were alluring. The cabin was small too for his creature. He ducked underneath my door when he went into my bedroom.

"Did you bring me a deer, too?" Bay called out.

"It's in the front of the house," Zambezi replied.

Bay excused himself, so he could eat, leaving me at the table.

Zambezi and Bay made a few changes to the cabin. Since the kitchen area was bigger, they knocked my wall out and redid it, making my room spacious. The floor wasn't dry rotting anymore because they replaced it. It was coming along nicely, and I couldn't wait to see the outcome since Zambezi planned on knocking more walls out to expand the cabin. When I went inside my bedroom, Zambezi was asleep and the blood on him was cleaned off. Since he was so tall, he threw out my small bed and brought in a bigger one where we both could fit. After taking off my clothes, I joined him. I laid on the far end of the bed to give him some space. As soon as I was ready to close my eyes, I heard arguing coming from outside.

"Zambezi!" I nudged him, but he wouldn't move. He was a very heavy sleeper. Sometimes I had to punch him to wake up and that didn't always work. He'd been working at his market and fixing the cabin; since he needed his rest I left him alone. I grabbed my robe and rushed outside. Deer body parts were everywhere. I cringed when I almost tripped over a deer's head. Zambezi ate like an animal. Bay was by the water with a woman. She was swinging at him, but he dodged her.

"Keep your hands to yourself! Why are you here? We're over!" he yelled at her.

"We're not over! I need you," she pleaded with Bay.

"I don't want you, now leave!" he shouted.

I walked closer to them and it was Laguna's sister, Ara. She slapped Bay's face, opening his skin.

"Leave him alone, bitch!" Ara's black eyes looked at me and her once brown complexion was turning gray. Her mouth was hideous, she had big swollen red gums with shark teeth.

"I'll scratch your pretty face," she said.

"What happened to you? Damn, you look like a hammerhead shark. Is this why the town is empty? Y'all practicing voodoo or something?" Bay asked. Ara slashed his chest and he fell over. I rushed to her and tackled her. She clawed at my face while my nails slashed through her flesh.

"Shore watch out!" Bay said. Someone appeared out of nowhere and kicked me in the head. I fell into the water, pulling a gray creature with me. It bit my arm and my teeth sharpened while expanding from my gums. They were too big for my mouth, putting pressure on my head. The creature screamed when I pulled off its arm with my teeth. We were sinking further down, while we fought and bit each other. The creature grabbed my locket, trying to pull it off my neck. The locket opened, and the creature exploded into chunky pieces. I swam up to the top and Bay was being attacked by four creatures, Ara included.

"Zambezi!" I called out while swimming back. When I made it on land, Bay turned into his creature and killed one of the gray fish people. Two creatures jumped into the lake, heading towards me. I dived under, swimming in their direction. Two long fish tails glowed underneath me. It was Reef and Rain. They attacked the sea creatures, tearing away at their flesh. I left them to check up on Bay. When I went above water, a big black dragon with blue and gold scales was shooting water from its mouth, stripping the creatures' flesh away from their bodies. Ara escaped, she disappeared into the woods. Reef and Rain came up from underneath with blood dripping from their teeth.

"That bitch was nasty," Reef said.

I swam away towards the land. My body was chasing after Ara and I wanted it to stop before it led us to trouble.

*Stop! They might kill me! Slow the hell down!*

I sniffed the air, smelling the scent of blood from Ara's wound—I became a monster. My body zipped through the woods, following her trail. Ara was human again, she was also injured. She screamed and begged me not to harm her when I caught her by the hair.

"STOP! Please stop!" she cried.

*Let her go, damn it! We've already killed!*

"I just wanted to get Bay away from the cabin. Please, Shore. I know this isn't what you want to do," she cried as I dragged her by the hair. Zambezi and Bay were in human form and they were arguing.

"Where is your mother hiding? That bitch sent them here!" Zambezi yelled at Bay. Rain and Reef were burying what was left of the gray creatures.

"Bayyyyy, help me!" Ara cried. She held her face and cried after I slid her into a rock. Zambezi placed his hand on my shoulder.

"Snap out of it," he whispered.

*I'm trying to!*

Bay went to Ara and she wrapped her arms around him.

"Adwoa made me come. She cursed us! I can't control that thing I was. We only came to get Caspian back. I was trying to distract you so the others could sneak in but that whore ruined it! We didn't want to fight," Ara said to Bay.

"NOOOO!" Bay hollered when I slashed her throat.

"Damn it, Shore! You could've waited until she told us where Adwoa and the rest of them are hiding!" Zambezi said.

"You didn't have to kill her," Bay said, holding on to her body.

"Well, she's dead so now we will bury her," Rain said. Reef and Rain grabbed Ara's body to take to the pile. Bay went to the woods and Zambezi went into the lake. I went over to Rain and Reef to help them bury the bodies.

"Don't let them make you feel bad. Sometimes we turn into creatures that kill," Rain said.

"I can't control it. It seems as if something else is inside of me," I replied.

"We're all the same," she said.

"How did you know I was in trouble?"

"We were close by, looking for seashells. We can also sense it," Reef said.

We used our nails to dig up the dirt. Once the hole was big enough, we put the corpses in.

"These are people from the town. Adwoa must've turned them. We didn't know they were sea people," Rain said.

"That's because something else is going on. This town was normal until Shore showed up," Reef said.

I walked away from them to open up my locket. When I asked it to show me Adwoa, nothing happened. It was almost as if she didn't exist.

"Why aren't you showing me her?"

The locket showed me nothing of Laguna or Ara when I asked. I was more confused than ever. Jewel said the locket was the eyes and ears of all the waters. If Adwoa was a part of the sea, it should've showed me. Zambezi came out of the water, Rain and Reef ran towards the lake.

"What are y'all doing?"

"He's crazy!" Reef said.

"I got y'all something," he said.

Rain and Reef walked over to us and Zambezi chuckled.

"I hope you're not setting us up. We'll attack you," Reef said.

Zambezi held his hand out. There were five seashells in his hand. They were the color of pearls. Rain snatched the shells from him. The way to a water fairy's heart was to bring her gifts.

"Where is mine?" I asked.

"Who cares. These are beautiful," Reef said.

"They are very nice. I can make an anklet with these," Rain said.

"I'm going to be the bigger person and apologize for not liking y'all but since y'all are Shore's sisters, then I'll be nice. But if I get pinched one more time, all the nice shit is off the table," Zambezi said.

Bay came out of the woods and Reef's eyes glowed. Rain rolled her eyes.

"I guess you can have him. I like older men anyway," Rain told Reef.

"You didn't have a choice. Now, excuse me. I'm going to make sure my little sea horse is fine," Reef said and went over to Bay.

"We'll come by later to check up on you. Goodnight," Rain said, walking towards the lake.

"Come on, Reef!" Rain called out.

"I'll see you later, baby. Just remember what I told you," Reef said to Bay.

"What, you scared?" Zambezi asked Bay after Reef joined Rain in the lake.

"Naw. I'm tapping that soon. But I'm going in to check on father," Bay said. He went into the cabin; it was just me and Zambezi outside.

"Thank you for doing that."

"I was being selfish, but I had my reasons. If you can get along with my brother and protect him, I can do the same for your sisters," he said. I jumped in Zambezi's arms and wrapped my legs around him.

"Laguna and others are going to come looking for Ara and the rest of the dead ones. So, we gotta prepare for the worst because it's just us against them," he said.

"Let's forget about all of it. I want you have it," I said referring to my virginity.

"You been through a lot tonight. We can talk about this when we wake up."

"I don't care about what just happened because we're still here. We don't need to wait. We're carved into each other's soul. What's to wait for?" I asked.

"We can't leave. What if they come back?" he asked, stalling.

"Let's grab some sheets from my bedroom and take me to your boat."

"Aight," he said.

I was nervous myself, but it seemed so right. The aching between my legs wasn't going away. Zambezi gave me pleasure every night with his tongue, but it didn't put out the fire. We went into the cabin and I grabbed a few things for the shower. Zambezi put a shower house behind the cabin. It was just a sprinkler with boards around it for privacy. My stomach was doing summersaults while heading back out the cabin to the shower. Zambezi joined me moments later.

"Why are you nervous?"

"It'll be my first time being with a virgin. I don't want to hurt you. My size might rearrange something," he said.

"I'm not scared of you."

"What are we waiting for? Let's hurry up then," he said.

We rinsed the soap off our bodies and Zambezi handed me a towel. Afterwards, we headed towards the boat. Zambezi laid sheets out then he told me to lay down. He laid on top of me and kissed me. Zambezi's erection was pressed against my swollen clit. Essence dripped from my slit while his hands cupped my pussy. He brushed his thumb across my slit while I called out his name.

"I'm ready to explode and I'm not inside of you yet," he groaned while playing in my slit. He wrapped my legs around him and those butterflies were pissing me off again. Zambezi gazed at my lips before tracing the outline of them with his tongue. He pushed himself forward, the tip of him was at my entrance. He slipped his tongue into my mouth and kissed me deeply, distracting me from the pain I was ready to feel. Each poke at my entrance hurt while trying to push his size into the tightness of me.

"SSSSSHHHHHH!" I hissed when the head of him was ripping me open. I burst into tears from the pain and Zambezi stopped.

"I can't do this," he said, pulling away. I grabbed his arm and told him to keep going.

"You sure?" he asked, and I nodded my head. He kissed the tears away while pushing further. The pain was worse than the first time. His size was stretching me, causing my legs to shake. He kissed my neck and my nails scratched at his back, breaking the skin.

"You feel so good," he groaned against my ear. Zambezi wasn't all the way inside me, so I could only imagine the torture. The strokes were starting to get deeper and by each second, more of his width was entering me. He was getting wider, swelling inside me. Zambezi massaged my breasts, squeezing my nipples between his fingers while sucking on my neck. Everything he was doing to my body was taking the pain away. His back dipped with each stroke and suddenly the feeling was starting to change. The boat was rocking, causing waves in the lake. Water splashed onto the boat, weighing it down.

"The boat is going to sink."

"Fuck this boat," he groaned, kissing my lips. Zambezi gripped my hips, his fingers firmly pressed into my skin, almost stuck. The waves picked up, rocking us harder. The tip of the boat was in the water and we were tilting. He gripped the side of the boat and pressed deeper. The veins in his dick were throbbing against my walls.

"UMMMMMMMMM! SHORE! FUCK!" he moaned while gripping my hair. Zambezi's dick vibrated, while his tongue was vibrating against my nipple. I accidentally scratched him, shredding the skin on his back.

"ARRGGHHHHHHHHHH!" I screamed.

The waves were coming up, splashing over us. The boat sank underneath the water and Zambezi held me close to him. We were changing. My legs were the same as Zambezi's, covered in silky scales. There was a tornado of fish swimming around us. The tip of Zambezi's locs interlocked with my hair. We landed on top of a rock, a thousand feet underneath the surface. Zambezi made love to me. He slammed into me, his body sent waves through mine, making me explode.

*I'm ready to explode. You're squeezing me, beautiful,* he thought.

Zambezi pumped harder and faster, my scales were scraping against the rock. He swelled, and the vibration tripled. That screeching, high-pitched noise escaped my lips, scaring the fish around us away. Zambezi exploded inside of me, filling me up. He laid on my chest and I hugged him, never wanting to let go. I was in love and it came out of nowhere. We fell asleep at the bottom of the lake.

# Adwoa

**Eight hours later...**

"Why hasn't my sister returned?" Laguna asked, entering the ship.

"I don't know but be my guest to go look for her."

Laguna knocked over the candle on my table. "Why did you send her?" she asked.

"Who are you to question me, child? Do you want to end up at the bottom of the swamp, so the bottom feeders can eat you?"

"We're going to die soon without blood!" she yelled.

"You all are going to die soon. I always find a way," I replied.

"What have you done to us?" she cried.

"Tears won't get you answers, Laguna, but shedding blood will. If you want to know why the others haven't returned, I suggest you get some people and go find them. As you can see, I'm busy praying to my goddess."

"You promised us beauty forever and wealth! And yet we have nothing! Those things we turn into are hideous and you are the ugliest one of all. We have been striving while worshipping Oceana and the water fairies! But your belief is ruining us!" she screamed. Laguna screeched when I grabbed her by the throat, lifting her off the ship's floor.

"Worshipping Oceana will kill you. She doesn't care about you humans! Oceana is a goddess to her kind, not yours! My goddess serves all and you will believe in her or get beheaded! You people couldn't survive without me! If it wasn't for me, Oland would've been taken by the humans and destroyed for buildings. You will not disrespect me!" I squeezed her neck. Blood dripped onto the floor from her neck as her legs dangled, then I dropped her. She fell onto the floor, holding her throat.

"My sister might be dead," she gasped.

"As she should be if she didn't do what I told her to do. I want my mate back and one of you will get him for me. If I have to leave this ship, I'll make candles out all of you pieces of shit!"

Laguna got up and ran off the ship. I picked up the mirror and looked at my reflection. I still had my youth, but my beauty wasn't going to last. Lesidi came on the ship and sat in front of me.

"I planted the underwear underneath Zambezi's sink at his market like you asked. But they left the market happy. They are falling in love, Adwoa," she said.

"I need his blood!"

"You need to die and take us with you because you've gone too far! I lost my child because of you! This town was fine before we stepped foot in it. Let them be happy, Adwoa. Give his mother happiness in death since you took it from her," Lesidi said.

"You're the one who killed his mother! Caspian's blood was the only blood to save us! Why aren't you thankful, huh? I saved you, gave your life!"

"You killed meeeeeee!" she screamed.

"I gave you life. You're the reason why I made a deal with Elonora. I wanted to save you and your baby. But you seem to forget things."

"It doesn't matter anymore about me but leave them alone, Elonora. And what about, Bay? You've ruined him and you're not even his real mother!" Lesidi said.

"SHUT UP!"

"I'm tired, Adwoa. I'm soooo tired. You are worse than the people who took us and chained us at the bottom of this ship that you don't want to destroy," she said.

"We were going to be slaves! What did you want for yourself and child, huh? To be a white man's whore? His bed wench? They would've sold the both of you and even whipped you. I saved us from it all!"

"Yet we're still slaves to something just as evil. And you took the people in this town and made them slaves, too. I know you don't want to accept this, but we're already dead. We drowned at the bottom of this ship," she said. I went to Lesidi and hugged her while she cried on my shoulder.

"We need to rest now, Adwoa," she said. I reached underneath my skirt and grabbed a knife. While humming a song we used to sing, I raised the knife. Lesidi gasped when I drove it into the back of her neck. She pulled away from me with blood tears and black eyes.

"You can rest now."

Lesidi's blood dripped down the cracks of the ship. It was time for her to rest. She didn't want to worship Elonora, the goddess who gave us life after death.

"Jordan!" I called out.

Jordan came into the bottom of the ship. He was eighteen years old. His grandparents were still in the town. They thought he left home to help me fix my cabin back in Oland, but I turned him, giving him the same gift Elonora gave to me.

"Take her somewhere and bury her."

"Yes, ma'am," he replied.

"Thank you, son."


The stairs creaked underneath my feet when I walked up to the upper-level. We were in a swamp area, miles away from Oland. It was time for us to migrate; Elonora wanted to spread her beliefs across the world.

The people of Oland were camping out in the swamp, cooking food over campfires. The older ones didn't have any purpose, so I left them in Oland because they were still humans. Once they died out, Oland humans wouldn't be anymore. The plan was to slowly wipe out the human race. I heard footsteps coming from behind me. He wrapped his arms around me and whispered romantic things in my ear.

"Come to bed," he said.

"I can't rest knowing that we might die soon. We're getting weak and they are getting stronger since they found someone who can use the locket. That locket holds the strength of the waters. It can see things they can't. If they learn the true name of us, they'll be able to see our truths."

"They'll die before it happens," he said.

He turned me around and kissed me. His eyes were filled with lust while staring into mine. He was the only man that looked past my outer beauty. Caspian never saw the ugly thing that was hidden inside me. But my lover saw it and he fell deeper in love with me.

"If Oceana remembers Elonora, the locket will show her. It will show her everything."

"Oceana doesn't remember anything. She's been on land for twenty years, you told me that. She's not a goddess anymore," he said. He kissed me again, passionately. He pressed his body against mine and I felt the hardness of him.

"You make me feel so beautiful."

"That's because you are. I love you," he said.

I unbuckled his shorts, freeing him of the lovely piece he had between his legs. Caspian was better in bed, but my lover treated me like a delicate flower. He pulled me into the dark corner of the ship, so we could be hidden. I took off the dress and he lifted me up.

"Ummmmm," I groaned when he entered my body. Even though he was special to me, he was worthless. The only cure was Zambezi. Capturing a sea dragon was an addiction, it gave me power and strength. Their blood was magical, it was the fountain of youth.

"I want you all to myself," he moaned against my ear, while pumping into me. My skin was changing, and my once beautiful hair was white and stringy. I pushed him away and ran down the stairs to look in the mirror. What stared back at me was the thing Elonora turned into.

"NOOOOO!" I screamed and smashed the mirror. I grabbed a candle from underneath the pile of old animal bones where I hid them. The candle was almost gone, and it was supposed to be for us all, but I couldn't chance it. The humans were replaceable. I had thousands of children over the years and could get a thousand more.

Once I lit the candle and inhaled its pungent scent, my beauty returned.

*Be patient, Adwoa. You'll have Zambezi soon...*

# Zambezi

**Two days later...**

S hore was sound asleep when I woke up. I was careful not to wake her. She was sleeping on her back with the sheet draped around her hips, exposing her succulent breasts. The tattoos on us had spread. It covered the entire left side of our bodies. It happened after she lost her virginity. Shore didn't have to say it, but the marking wasn't about me protecting her, it was about her mother stamping me for her daughter and as her lover, I was to keep her safe. The picture was clear as ever, but I had to figure out a way to persuade her to move into the beach house and still visit Lake Deep. The beach house was near the ocean which was bigger for me to maneuver around. Lake Deep seemed too small for my dragon because he wasn't finished growing, he was still considered an adolescent.

After getting dressed, I walked out the bedroom. Bay was fixing our father a vitamin drink. He'd been quiet since Shore killed Ara.

"Good morning, bro. I have to go into town today. Can you hold the fort down while I'm gone?"

"Naw, I can't. Let me go into town with you. Come on, bro. You treat me like a child. You're no better than Adwoa," he said. Perhaps, he was right. Bay wasn't a baby, but I couldn't live with myself if something happened to him.

"Those things might be everywhere."

"Exactly, so let me go with you. Shore can handle herself," he said.

The bedroom door to Shore's room opened. She came out wearing shorts and one of my T-shirts. Her hair was everywhere, and her eyes looked sleepy. I wanted her to get rest since I'd been inside of her for the past few days. I couldn't get enough of her.

"Whoa, you need a comb," Bay said, and she flicked him the finger. I smoothed her hair out and she was agitated.

"What? I'm trying to fix what I messed up."

"Y'all been fucking on each other and I have to hear it. I wish I could get some ass, too, but she killed my girlfriend and Reefa is playing around. She keeps teasing me and shit," Bay said.

"It's Reef and she's just trying to lure you in," Shore said.

"What about the other one? Rain? I think I like her," Bay said.

"You're too young for her, bro," I chuckled.

"She'll think twice once I taste her," Bay said.

"Ewww," Shore giggled.

"I want them all to take me advantage of me, bro. Even the old one, Jewel. The one you said was bomb and had nice breasts," Bay said to me.

"Would you shut the fuck up?" I gritted.

"You have been checking out my aunt?" Shore asked with her hands on her hips.

"Never."

"I'm going to the lake. I'll be right back," she said and left the cabin.

"Bro, you gonna end up knocking her up," Bay said.

I hadn't thought about that. I'd been so wrapped up in Shore that I wasn't pulling out. We had many years ahead of us and it was something I wasn't ready for. Honestly, I never thought about having kids.

"Naw, we ain't doing that. Besides, stay out of grown folks' business."

"I'm just saying," he shrugged.

"How is Father?"

"He's still the same. Go and see him. You barely check on him," Bay replied.

"I will later. I'm not in the mood right now. It's hard digesting what father has become. It's only three of us left—three! If he dies, that leaves just me and you. I'm tired of hearing that bullshit and seeing him cry like a sissy. If I go back there, I might drag him out of the bed and make him stand up."

"That's harsh, bro," he replied.

"Yeah, life be like that sometimes. I'll be back."

"I'm coming with you," Bay said.

"Naw, because you'll get soft if Adwoa shows up and she's the enemy."

"What if she's sick? We still need to help her. What if someone is making her do these things?" Bay asked.

"This is why you need to stay here."

Bay went into our father's room with a cup of herbs. I left out of the cabin and Shore was sitting on the rock by the lake, sun bathing her fish tail. Her thick green hair shimmered underneath the sun and her skin was of golden hue. She was humming while looking into a mirror. I didn't understand the fascination the water fairies had with mirrors. Her reef sisters were swimming in the lake. I couldn't see their faces, but I counted four tails waving out of the water. Bay came outside with a bottle of brown liquor in his hand.

"It's too early to drink."

"We're about to party, bro. Matter of fact, I'll wait here while you do what you have to do," he said. He sat the bottle on the ground and rushed towards the lake. When he jumped in, the water fairies rushed to him. Shore waved at me and I waved back before going into the woods.

***********

The town of Oland was quiet. The music they usually played wasn't as loud as it used to be and some of the markets were closed. The small houses also seemed empty.

"Excuse me, young man. How is Caspian feeling? I heard he was sick. Tell him Koretta asked for him. The town hasn't been the same since your father has fallen ill. He helped make this place a better one," an older black woman said.

"Appreciate it, I'll tell him."

She gave me a hug then walked into the bakery shop. Cascade's home he shared with his parents was only around the corner from my father's market. It'd been a while since I last saw him. I wanted to be certain that he didn't join Adwoa's clan. When I made it to his house, his mother was in her yard watering the flowers. She was an older woman, around age sixty-five. She and her husband took Cascade in when he was a baby. His parents left Oland and never looked back, leaving him with his grandparents to raise.

"Hi, Zambezi. How are you? I was getting worried about you," she said. She reached her arms out for a hug and I hugged her. She was a small, frail woman.

"I'm good, just came to check on Cascade."

"Oh, well, he's in the kitchen gutting fish. The door is unlocked," she said. I thanked her and headed towards the front door. All the cabin-style homes in Oland were small, only two bedrooms, but most of the them they had one. Even though it wasn't many people in Oland, the town was still too small for them which is why they couldn't use vehicles, just horses or bicycles. Cascade was in the kitchen, chopping up fish.

"Damn, bro. You a house wife now?" I teased from behind. He gave me dap when he turned around.

"I see you got jokes. Where the hell have you been and what's this I hear about your father closing down the market?" he asked.

"We've been having family issues so that's why I haven't been out. The market will open back up once things get back to normal again. But, what's up? You've been working out or something? You got swole on me."

"Yeah, with your father's market being closed, we had to make our own stand, so I have to do a lot of lifting. I heard you and the new girl are pretty close. Have you been hitting it?" he asked.

"She's important to me so I'm not gonna speak that way about her and you shouldn't either." Cascade held his hands up in defense.

"Whoa, my bad. We usually share information. But she hasn't been here long and she's important already?" he asked.

"I didn't know there was a time limit. I'm done talking about that though, what's up with the town?"

"I don't know. A lot of people left in the middle of the night. Now it's just me and the older ones," he shrugged. I was listening to his thoughts, wondering if he was going to give himself away. But I guess it didn't matter, Adwoa's thoughts never revealed her truth. If he was a part of them, I had to figure out a way to expose him.

"You're the only young one left?"

"No, it's a few others. Why, you heard something?" he asked.

"No, did you?"

"What's going on with you? Is everything aight?" he asked.

"Yeah, I'm straight. You want to go out tonight? Everything is on me since we haven't partied in a minute."

"Okay, cool. I don't have nothing to do tomorrow so we can do whatever," he said.

*Tell me about Adwoa!*

His mind was still blank, even after I got into his head again. Usually, I was able to make humans do what I wanted after hypnotizing them as they looked into my eyes. But I got nothing— maybe he didn't know about Adwoa.

"I'll holla at you later."

"Do you want to take some of this fish with you?" he asked.

"Naw, I'm straight."

We dapped again before I left his cabin.

*I wonder how Shore will feel if I go to the club? It's been a minute since I hung out.*

# Shore

"**W**atch out!" I shouted at Rain because Bay was ready to pull her underneath.

We were playing around in the lake. Bay joined us and couldn't stay away from Rain. She pretended not to like him, but they were flirting. Darya and Lake playfully attacked Bay and pushed him under the water. Reef was leaning against the rock, floating on her back while splashing water with her tail. She was silent which wasn't like her.

"What's bothering you?"

"I'm fine!" she said.

"Why are you so quiet?"

"Because I'm not in the mood," she said.

"Is it about Bay and Rain?"

"She's a bitch! She knew I liked him, really liked him. She wanted him for sex and I thought I did, too, until I finally got to see him close up. Now, look at them," Reef said.

"Maybe you should tell her."

"There is no point in telling her. Rain is prettier than me. No matter how much I look in the mirror and tell myself how beautiful I am, I can't compete with that. Aunt Jewel once told me that water dragons pick the prettiest ones," Reef replied.

"I think you're beautiful and maybe someone else is for you out there. Besides, I don't think Bay can handle you," I said.

"Now you're gonna make me cry," she said and rolled her eyes.

The door to the cabin opened and it was Zambezi's father. He was naked, and blood dripped from his mouth. He tripped and rolled down the small hill where the cabin sat. Bay got out of the water and rushed to him. I grabbed my shirt off the rock and put it over my head before getting out of the water. Zambezi gave me hell when I walked out of the water naked. I rushed to Caspian and he was choking on his blood.

"I saw her! She was here!" Caspian said.

"Who?"

"Adwoa, she was inside the room. She's desperate for blood. She came in through my window," he said. Me and Bay helped him up and took him back inside the cabin. Caspian didn't have a window in his room so maybe he was hallucinating because he was getting close to death. Bay laid him on the bed and Caspian reached out to me.

"I'm sorry for everything I've done," he said before closing his eyes.

"FATHER! WAKE UP!" Bay shouted, shaking him.

My reef sisters came inside the cabin, peeking into the room.

"We can take him to Jewel. She might not be able to save him, but she knows good remedies," Lake said.

"No, he has to stay here. He can't breathe underneath water anymore," Bay said.

"One of us can breathe into his mouth while travel," Darya said.

"It's not safe here for him anymore. We don't know what to do. Maybe Jewel knows, she's been around for a very long time," I replied.

"Let's hurry up and get him there before he dies," Lake said.

Bay wrapped his father's body in a sheet, so he could take him to the reef sister's mansion.

"We need to tie something around him so the pressure from the water doesn't knock him off," Rain said.

"There is rope outside," I replied.

We followed Bay outside and Darya grabbed the rope. She tied Caspian to Bay's body.

"Aight, follow us," Lake said.

They went into the lake and I followed them. Once we got further out into the deep part, we dived underneath, swimming through the blue water while the fish in the lake surrounded us.

\*\*\*\*\*\*\*\*\*\*\*

"We're going to get him settled in a room. Shore, go down the hall and tell Jewel we have a visitor," Rain said while they carried Caspian's long body up the spiral stairs. I ran down the hall of the mansion to the pool room where Jewel spent most of her time. Instead of knocking, I barged in. She was at the end of the pool, sipping her sea wine while the fish plucked at her tail.

"We need your help!" I panted.

"Why do you need my help when you have the power inside of your locket? I'm retired, Shore. Whatever it is, you can handle it," she said politely.

"It's Caspian, Zambezi's father. He's dying, and we brought him here, so you can help him."

"You brought Caspian to my home?" she asked.

"He's upstairs."

Jewel raised her tail out of the pool and then it disappeared. She grabbed her silk pink robe off her chair and tied it around her body.

"I want him out of my fucking house!" she screamed.

"What in the fuck is going on? We're all sea people! He needs our damn help. I know about him having a vendetta towards us but he's dying, and he knows he's been wrong."

"Get him out of my house or I'll kill him myself! You might be the princess of the waters and maybe a little naïve but I'm the queen of this castle! Don't make me kill him because I will," she said while her nails curved into hooks.

"You don't know what you just did to me!" Jewel said with tears falling from her eyes. She stormed past me and out of the pool room. I followed behind Jewel, shouting for her to calm down as she ran up the stairs. She sniffed the air, following his scent.

"JEWEL, STOP!" I yelled after her. She ran into the room where they took Caspian. She slapped him in the face while he was lying down. Her nails left nasty claw marks on his skin so Bay pressed the sheet against Caspian's cheek. Jewel's teeth expanded, turning into sharp thin needles. She jumped on top of Caspian and Bay slammed her on to the floor. The reef sisters sat on top of Jewel to calm her while me and Bay rushed to Caspian. Jewel's screams shattered the glass windows like dust and the ceiling trembled. Bay fell on to the floor holding his ears and Caspian's ears bled. I went over to Jewel and slapped her face.

"STOP IT!"

"I'll beat your ass if you touch Jewel like that again!" Lake said.

"You don't want to go there with me, Lake. Don't tempt me."

Jewel stopped screaming and ran out of the room. The reef sisters chased after her. While Bay tended to his father's wound, I went to check up on Jewel. They were in the hallway calming her down. She wasn't like herself. Jewel was headstrong and full of life. I admired her because of her strength but I wondered what made her snap.

"I'm sorry, Jewel, but I can't let you kill him. Please just have a heart and help him."

"That man is heartless. He doesn't care about nothing but a woman's body. I never wanted to see him again which is why I never stepped foot in Oland. I hate him!" she seethed.

"This was a bad idea," Rain said.

"I cannot believe we are having a debate about this. He's still considered one of us despite the difference of our kind. We shouldn't be separated."

"Just because you're fucking one of them doesn't mean Jewel should accept them," Lake said.

"Leave her alone, Lake! Shore is right, they are water people, too," Rain said. Lake went into a room down the hall and slammed the door.

"Fine, I'll do it. But after I help him, I want him gone!" Jewel said. She went down the spiral staircase and I went inside the bedroom with Caspian.

"He doesn't have much blood left," Bay said while wiping his forehead.

"Jewel is going to help him. She was just angry about a quarrel they had a long time ago."

"I hope so because if not, I'm leaving and getting away from that crazy bitch," Bay said.

Caspian coughed and wheezed. I didn't know why I cared so much about his well-being. Maybe it was because I knew what it was like to be sick and dying. Jewel came back into the room with a bucket of jelly fish.

"What is that going to do?" Bay asked.

"Numb him from the pain. Giva should be home soon, she traveled to the Mediterranean Sea for healing herbs. Once she gets back, she can help him. This will preserve him. Keep him from dying fast," she said. Jewel placed the jelly fish on top of Caspian's body and they stung him. He froze in shock.

"You killed him!" Bay said to Jewel.

"Child, don't speak to me that way!" Jewel said.

"This will slow down whatever is killing him. I'm saving is pathetic life," Jewel said. She pulled away from Caspian and Bay covered him up.

"You can stay here until Giva returns. Make yourself at home but we don't have what you eat," Jewel said to Bay. I followed her out the room to thank her, but she held a blank expression.

"I hope Caspian never betrays you, too. If he does, I'm going to kill him and return the slap you gave me. You better have this under control. Now, excuse me, we're having a party tonight and I have to get ready. You might as well stay until then," she said. Jewel went back down the stairs and I sat in a chair in the hallway. My locket opened, and water spilled onto the floor. The light in the hallway faded away and the bedroom doors disappeared. I was back home inside my cabin.

*What in the hell just happened?* I thought, looking around.

The cabin was back to the same way it was when me and my mother first moved in. Caspian came out of the bedroom with a bloody baby while I heard screams coming from the back room. I rushed to the back and Jewel was laying on the floor with her stomach cut open. I covered my mouth to keep from screaming at the gruesome scene.

"Jewel!" I called out, but she couldn't hear me.

"Bring me my baby!" Jewel screamed at Caspian. He came back into the room with the baby wrapped in a blanket.

"What we did was a mistake, Jewel. You and I both know your reef sisters wouldn't forgive you for what you did, especially to Harbor. Let me keep him and I'll find someone to help me raise him. You need to leave this cabin now," he said. Jewel crawled to him, reaching up for her baby.

"Please, don't do this to me!" she screamed.

"I don't want my son to deal with what Zambezi went through. He will not be raised in the waters! You know what happened to your sister, so you should want what is best for him," Caspian said.

"I thought you loved me. I forgave you for bedding my reef sister and choosing her behind my back while I was away! I forgave the both of you and never lost love for neither one of you, but I'm begging you to please give me my son," Jewel cried. Caspian's eyes watered but he didn't let the tears fall.

"I met someone else. She will help me raise my sons. I'm moving out," Caspian said.

"Oceana was right about you! Your heart is cold-blooded, just like the nasty reptile you are! You're only doing this because Oceana left the waters. If she was here, she would have ripped out your tongue," Jewel said.

"But she's not here and that locket you have of hers doesn't work for you!" Caspian said before leaving the cabin. Jewel laid on the floor and cried. Then suddenly, the image faded away. The surroundings changed, and I was back at Jewel's mansion.

*So that's how she ended up near Oland. She left the sea to secretly give birth. What have I done? Bringing Caspian here was a smack in the face to her. He treated her badly and he took his son away from her.*

Bay was sitting in the chair falling asleep while cupping himself because he was naked. I had to find him some clothes, so he could get comfortable. While staring into his face, I could see the resemblance between him and Jewel. He had her nose and lips but he still looked like his father. My heart changed for Caspian. I hated him and no longer cared if they saved him or not. Everything that was happening to him was because of the wicked things he did.

### Nine hours later...

It was getting late and I was still at the mansion, preparing for Jewel's party. Rain and Reef were combing my hair while I stared into the mirror. They were gossiping about Jewel, wanting to know why she snapped. I kept my mouth shut about the images I saw. It wasn't my place to gossip about Jewel's heartbreak.

"They are here!" Darya called out from the hallway.

"You look amazing," Rain said to me.

I was wearing a short black dress with a pair of spike heels. The dress was a little too revealing but it was the only piece of clothing Rain had that fit me.

"I look like a two-dollar hooker."

"Stop overreacting," Reef said.

I sprayed a little perfume on my neck before following Reef and Rain out of the bedroom. We went downstairs, and the music was playing. There were around ten guys standing in the foyer. Lake pranced around in her see-through dress while they drooled over her. I felt uncomfortable at the stares I was given. Zambezi was the only one who could look at me that way.

"Wow, I wasn't expecting to see you here," a voice said from behind me. When I turned around, I was greeted by Nerida. He was wearing white shorts with a silk top and a pair of expensive sneakers.

"I should've known you were one of us," he said. When he extended his hand out to me, it was covered in scales.

"Nice seeing you again," I said while looking around. The reef sisters were mingling in with the male guests.

"Is your boyfriend here?" he asked.

"No, he's not here."

"Well, come over here and meet my brothers," Nerida said. He grabbed my hand and led me to a group of men. Most of them had an island accent.

"You look amazing," one of them said to me while eyeing my breasts. Rain told me about the parties they had but it was my first time attending one. Darya was passing around a tray of sea wine. When Bay came down the stairs, dressed in gym shorts and socks, everyone looked at him. I stepped away from Nerida so he wouldn't get the wrong idea. The men stared at Bay, grilling him. His masculinity put an elephant in the room. He was taller and more defined.

"I bet he works on a farm," I heard one of them whisper.

"He does look a little poor," another one said.

Bay took a glass of sea wine off the tray and guzzled it. After he was finished, his loud burp bounced off the walls of the mansion.

"This party is dry and very fairyish," Bay said, grabbing another drink. After he was finished, he went back upstairs, unfazed by the evil stares.

"What else do you do besides work at that fish house?" Nerida asked.

"Screw my boyfriend at the bottom of the lake," I stated rudely. They were all annoying me with their boastful attitudes and snide remarks about Bay. Lake pulled me to the side after overhearing me and Nerida.

"These men are rich, Shore. I get that you like to play house with your water dragon and he has good sex, but these are practically millionaires. Nothing is wrong with having a little fun," Lake said. She disliked Zambezi because of the things he said to her, so she was always negative about my relationship.

"I'm loyal to Zambezi. We're made for each other." Lake threw her head back in laughter.

"You cannot seriously think after a little time with him that you're made for each other. Maybe the symbols come from something else. I mean you're pretty much the little princess of the waters and you want to waste it on a sea dragon who owns fish markets? These men own restaurants all over the world. Just use one of them," Lake whispered.

"I think you need to let what Zambezi said to you go because you're starting to become ugly. Lately, you have been making my ass itch. I don't care if Zambezi lived underneath a rock, I'll still give my heart to him."

"You're making a big mistake," Lake spat before she walked off.

I walked outside through the back door in the kitchen area. The small beach was littered with bottles and other things. The land was pretty much abandoned and not taken care of.

"What are you doing out here?" Jewel asked when she stepped out of the shadows.

"I'm not into the partying thing."

"That's because you're not a regular fairy. Come have a drink with me," she said. I sat on an old beach chair next to Jewel. The waves brushed up on the shore and the breeze was blissful.

"I saw what happened," I blurted out.

"I know you did. The locket shows what you want to know but I don't like to talk about that day," she said.

"Bay is your son, Jewel. He thinks Adwoa is his mother."

"He's better off without me," she said and took a sip from her bottle before passing it to me.

"I hope you tell him one day. If Caspian dies, he won't have a parent. Adwoa isn't good news. Do you know why the locket doesn't show her?"

"The locket only shows what's a part of the waters. If she's not one us, then she's something

else. Maybe she's a part of a swamp," Jewel
joked.

"What about the swamps?"

"Your mother once told me her locket shows
her all the waters except for the swamps. We can
go anywhere but there. She taught me many
things and because of her, I was able to rule the
waters. Enough about that, how are you and
Zambezi coming along?" she asked.

"Great! He's my best friend before anything.
He even taught me how to swim."

"You wouldn't have to learn if you were born
in the waters. For many years, I hated that boy. I
know it's not his fault but he's a constant
reminder of what Caspian and Harbor did. But I
had a change of heart for him when he came to
the bottom of the lake for you the day the waters
healed you. I can understand why Oceana wanted
him to protect you. Be careful, though, love hurts
sometimes," Jewel said. I took another sip of the
wine while leaning back in the chair. There was a
bolt of lightning sailing through the sky.

"There he goes," Jewel smiled.

"The man in the sky?"

"Yes," she said.

"What if it's a woman?"

"I believe it's a man. It's just something about that lightning bolt. You know the humans make a wish when they see a falling star. I wonder if it's real," Jewel said.

"Just a myth."


Jewel reminded me of my mother. Both drank a lot to ease the pain yet were still very strong. Instead of going back inside the house with the rest of the sisters, I sat outside with Jewel and watched the stars.

# Zambezi

I waited at the lake for hours for Shore, Bay and my father. Pissed off was an understatement. There weren't any signs of someone else on the property and everything inside the cabin was intact.

"This is some bullshit!"

It was almost eleven o'clock at night and Cascade was sitting at the kitchen table, dressed to go out. I was still wearing what I had on earlier.

"They might've taken him to a hospital or something. I mean he was sick, and we don't have real doctors here, just herb doctors. Loosen up and get dressed before the club closes," Cascade said.

"Go ahead and go. I gotta stay here in case something bad happened. Maybe I can find her."

"I came here for nothing," Cascade said.

"The clubs aren't going anywhere."

I walked outside and went to the lake, hoping they showed up soon.

"I'm leaving. I'll catch you some other time," Cascade said from behind me.

"Aight, be safe!"


I went to Shore's favorite rock to watch the lake. She wasn't supposed to just leave without me knowing considering what was going on with Oland. I didn't even know for sure if she was with Bay or my father. Since me and Shore have been kicking it, I lost the love I once had with the inner-cities. The human girls I used to sleep with became a distant memory. I couldn't think of their names, even if I tried. While I was in deep thought, I heard something rustling in the bushes. I rushed over, hoping it was Shore or Bay. A girl, maybe around age eighteen or nineteen, stumbled out of the woods and fell onto the grass. Her white dress was muddy and stained with blood. When I turned her over, blood leaked from her neck.

"Adwoa is-she's in the sw—amp," she stuttered.

"Where? We don't have any swamps in this area."

"It's hi—dden behind an old ship. Miles away from here," she gasped. She choked on her blood and bugs were crawling on her. I picked her up and rushed her to the lake to clean her off. When I jumped into the water, she held on to me.

"Pleaassseee, don't drown me," she screamed.

I dipped her underneath the water three times and the big water bugs fell off her. She was weak and frail, and her ankles had scars around them, the same scars as Adwoa's. I took her out the water and laid her on the ground.

"I ne—edd your blood so I ca—annn hel—p you," she said.

"Need my blood? Is this a setup?" I pulled away from her and she reached out to me.

"You can ki—ill me af—ter I tell yo—uuu he—r truth," she choked.

I picked her up and grabbed an old rope by the house. I tied the stranger to a tree, just in case she was tricking me.

"Why don't you need a candle?"

"It's to cont—roll," she said.


The stranger opened her mouth while I ripped the skin off my forearm with my teeth. The blood dripped down her throat. The veins in her body were protruding through her skin. Her black eyes turned the colors of the waters before she passed out. The wound on her neck healed and her frail body filled out. I didn't know our blood was capable of healing, I thought it was used as voodoo instead. She was out for about an hour before she opened her eyes. The stranger broke away from the tree to feel her neck.

"Don't try anything stupid!"

She fell into my arms and wrapped her arms around me. I pulled her away. "No need for that. Tell me what I want to know."

"Adwoa worships a sea demon. It tricked her many years ago. It came to her, disguised as a water fairy. We were dying when she came to us. She saved us but only so we could do her dirty work. I still don't have all the answers, but I know Adwoa tricked the people of Oland, made them believe she was Oceana and now they worship her because she promised them wealth, beauty and eternal life. She wants you next, so she can use your strength and blood to keep her pretty," she said.

"Take me to her."

"I can't. It's too many of them hiding in the waters of the swamp, waiting to kill anything that gets close. I'm telling you to warn you. She wants you to submit to her, so she can seduce you, weaken your mind and drain you until she finds another of your kind," she said.

"Why my kind?"

"I just told you why!" she said.

"You know what I mean. What's special about our blood?"

"Your kind sheds skin to remain youthful, to grow and even to gain more strength. It's like renewing yourself into a better one. I guess you can see why we need it. I never wanted any of this. For years I've watched Adwoa trick many men of your kind until they began dying out. She kills their mates first then seduces them when they're grieving. She does all of this to stay beautiful like a fairy," she said.

"Shore is her next victim?"

"She has the locket. It won't be that easy and she knows it," she said.

"This is some straight bullshit. I can't believe that muthafucka is doing all of this, so she can be pretty? Who does shit like that? Never mind, I saw what they turn into and I'm saying, they can't hold a candle to a slug."

The stranger dropped her hand into her hands and sobbed.

"My bad, I wasn't calling you ugly."

"It's okay. I know what I can turn into. But my heart is still pure. I'd rather die than live this life. I stood by Adwoa and watched her sink many slave ships for the ones who believed in Oceana. She freed them but not in a good way. The others, she let drown, forgetting she was once one of them. I feared her for so long and hated myself because I was weak until Shore came to Oland. Shore is our only hope since Oceana doesn't exist anymore," she said.

"How did you escape?"

"After Adwoa stabbed me, I pretended I was dead. One of her worshippers buried me in the mud and I waited hours until I crawled out my grave. I was still dying then but I had to find someone. I didn't know how to get here since Adwoa made me stay in the swamp all these years, so I had to ask someone about Lake Deep. The humans in Oland wanted me to come into their home so they could help me, but I didn't have time to waste," she said.

"What's your name?" I asked

"Lesidi."

"I can bring you some clothes. I'll be back."

I rushed into the cabin and grabbed one of Shore's nightshirts. Shore had a good heart, so I knew she wouldn't mind. While I was grabbing cups for water, the door to the cabin opened. She came into the cabin and looked around. Her dirty feet left footprints on the floor. She sniffed around the place and touched things she must not have been familiar with.

"I've never been inside a home before. Adwoa always kept me outside. I hope I don't trouble you," she said. Lesidi looked even younger since I healed her. Her skin was the color of coffee beans and her face was round and small. Her hair was braided down her back and she was petite.

"What age were you when Adwoa made a sacrifice?"

"Eighteen, I think. I can't remember, I just know I was pregnant with my third child. My husband at the time had four wives, I was the youngest. That's all I remember," she yawned.

"You can lie down in the bed in the back room."

Lesidi went into the room and peeled off her dress. She stood in the doorway naked and I turned my head. I sat at the kitchen table, reaching for Bay's liquor bottle. My head was throbbing, and my body temperature rose.

*First Shore, Bay and my father goes missing now I have a woman sleeping in Shore's cabin after crawling out of a grave. This is one of the reasons why I need to get out of Oland. The shit was all bad for us...*

**The next day...**

I woke up to a kiss on my cheek. When I opened my eyes, Shore was standing in front of me naked. My head was pounding from the liquor since I wasn't big on drinking moonshine. My throat was dry, and I was seeing double vision. The clock on the wall read, one o'clock. The sun was shining outside so that meant Shore stayed out all night.

"Wake up," she said, kissing me again.

"Yo, get the fuck off of me!" I spat while pushing away from the table.

"I did something wrong?"

"How in the hell can you be gone all day and come home like shit is good?"

"Your father got sicker and we took him to Jewel's house so Giva could try to help him. I'm sorry I stayed out late," she said. Shore reeked of alcohol and weed. I wanted to be more understanding, but I wasn't into the new her. I had feelings for her, but staying out late, getting high and drunk wasn't my thing, especially since she wasn't a virgin anymore. All I could think about was Shore giving a man what she gave to me.

"So, that muthafucka more important than me?"

*Damn, I'm jealous as fuck right now.*

"No, but he's your father! I thought that's what you would want!" she yelled at me.

"You should've left a fucking note then! You still ain't answer my question, though. Why you ain't return home last night? It takes a whole day to swim to Jewel's house?"

"They had a party and I sat and talked to Jewel. It was innocent! I don't know why you're coming at me like this," she said.

"Y'all had men there, too, huh?"

"Yeah, but I was outside with Jewel!" she said. Shore was shaking, she was on the verge of crying. Maybe I was coming at her too strong, but I basically threw away my plans to be with her. Falling in love with her just came out of nowhere and it knocked me back—so far back that I didn't know who the hell I was anymore.

"Yo, you smell like a strip club. You want me to believe you wasn't turning up with your sisters? That's all you do, drink, smoke and look into those damn mirrors like your face is going to change every five minutes!"

"You're overreacting because you think I was with someone else! Ask your brother when he comes home. I would never disrespect you," she said.

"You just did, though. Your sisters are practically whores. You're the only one who has someone. You think they respect me? I know one of your trout face sisters tried to talk to you into fucking with someone else."

Shore grew silent, perhaps I was telling the truth. It was to the point where I didn't want to get inside her head in fear I might fly off the walls. The door to the spare bedroom opened and Lesidi came out, naked and rubbing her eyes. I forgot she was inside the cabin.

"Ohhhhh, so this is reverse psychology? You accused me of cheating, yet you have a whore in my cabin?" she asked. Shore's eyes turned, and spiky scales pierced through her skin; she felt threatened.

"I think you might want to run, Lesidi, and you better haul ass!" Lesidi stood there with a blank expression on her face. Shore jumped on me, her long nails ripping through my skin, and I grabbed her arms. She bit a chunk out of my shoulder and Lesidi jumped on Shore's back.

"Stay out of it, Lesidi!"

"Leave him alone!" Lesidi yelled. Shore snatched her off by the hair and tossed her across the cabin.

"Baby calm down! It's not what you think!" My blood was splashing on the walls. I bit her arm to get her off me. The monster inside me was fighting to break through and rip her throat out.

"Shore get off me!" I bellowed. My voice was changing, and scales and rough skin stretched across my body. An electric wave shocked her, and she fell into the wall. She was ready to attack me again but Lesidi intervened. She tackled Shore onto the floor and they had a brawl.

"I can't let you hurt him! He saved me!" Lesidi said. Shore slammed her head into the wall, putting a hole in it. I broke up the fight and was getting hit in the midst of it. To stop them from tearing up the cabin, I took them outside. I pulled Lesidi away and tossed her into the lake then I grabbed Shore and took her into the cabin. She kicked and was ready to scream but I covered her mouth, clutching her face tightly so she wouldn't destroy anything.

"Calm the hell down!"

She was breathing rapidly, tiring herself out while I held her against the wall. Shore turned back to her normal self. When she turned into that creature, she couldn't control it—she wasn't herself.

"I can't believe you," she said.

"I don't know her, I just met her last night. I know I have a history of sleeping with a lot of women, but I promise you I didn't touch her. She came here to warn us about Adwoa and she needs our help to get rid of her. Lesidi was damn near dead and I let her rest. I couldn't send her back out there like that."

Shore pulled away from me and went inside her bedroom. She came back out moments later.

"Where are my fish? Please tell me you have our fish?"

"I don't know what you're talking about!"

"My fucking fish are gone! The fish that represents us and our destiny! Where are they? They were a gift from the waters. That bitch tricked you! They took my fish and probably separated them, so we could fight, and you fell for it. I want you out of my cabin!" she said.

"Yo, you're fuckin' crazy! Lesidi wouldn't tell me their secrets if she wanted to trick me. Why would she stay here, sleep in your cabin, if she had something to do with it? That would be too obvious, and nobody is that damn stupid!"

"You're just like your piece of shit father! I'm done with you!"

Shore left out of the cabin and rushed to the lake. I didn't want to chase her because we both needed space. I watched her dive underneath the water and just like that, she was gone. Lesidi came from behind a tree.

"I didn't mean to attack her. She was trying to kill you," she said.

I left Shore's cabin and went into the woods, heading back to my old cabin. Lesidi followed me while apologizing over fifty times. Once we made it to my father's old property, I told her she could stay in his old cabin. It wouldn't be right of me if I invited her into mine. She was well rested and able to fend for herself.

"Is that where Adwoa used to live?" she asked.

"Yeah, but I doubt if she's coming back. Go in there and put on some clothes. Do not knock on my door or disturb me unless it's an emergency."

"I'll apologize to Shore when I see her again. I'm going to make her a necklace, she'll love that," she said. She went inside the cabin and I went into mine.

*What just happened between me and Shore? Does she really think those fish are important to us?* I thought while heading to the shower room. Even though our relationship was short-lived, it left a big impact on me when she told me it was over. Now I was stuck trying to figure out a way to live without her.

# Bay

**Two days later…**

"**S**top being grumpy and take the drink!" Giva yelled at my father. After he woke up from a deep sleep, he refused any care from the water fairies. My father turned his head. The drinks Giva made was to help my father's body reproduce more blood since he lost a lot, but he couldn't stand the taste.

"Help me out, child. Don't just stand there and look. This is your father," Giva said. I knew Giva from Oland. She came into town like three days a week to sell peaches and herbs at her stand. I didn't know she was a water fairy until she came to Jewel's home.

"Chill, Father!" I said while pressing down his arms. Giva forced the drink down his throat and he choked.

"Toughen up, big guy. A little fish shit ain't going to hurt you," Giva said.

"Go to hell," my father said.

"Fuck off, weak man," Giva laughed while walking out of the room.

"Why do they hate you? Jewel and Giva?"

"Because they just do. Where is your brother?" he asked.

"Back at the lake I guess."

"Get me out of here. Do it now or you'll be punished!" he yelled.

"Why do you want to die so badly? Is being a father that hard of a job? Aren't you the man me and Zambezi are supposed to look up to? This is embarrassing!"

"You'll hate me if I live. I've done a lot of bad things and I can't stop thinking about them. Every time I close my eyes, I see Harbor. Your brother is more of a man than I am, let him guide you. I want to see Harbor again. That's all I want," he said.

"Harbor wouldn't want you to let her son down. The way you talk about her, I know she had a loving spirit and wouldn't want this for your family."

Jewel knocked on the door before she came in. She had a plate of raw meat in her hand.

"Eat," she said, handing me the food.

"How did you catch this?" I asked.

"A long time ago, I used to catch food to satisfy my lover. I have my ways," she said. I took the food from her and my father reached for the meat. Jewel smacked his hand.

"I didn't catch that for you. If you want meat, get your ass up and get it!" she said.

"This isn't going to make me regret anything, Jewel. Give it up," my father said.

Jewel left out of the room and slammed the door behind her. I gave my father half of my meat and he devoured it. His appetite was coming back.

"Why do you talk to Jewel that way? She let you stay in her home."

"You're too young to understand," he said.

He turned to his side, his back towards me, which meant he was done talking to me. I left the room and went downstairs. The house was quiet which meant the water fairies went to the city or swimming. I headed to the pool room at the end of the hallway to swim. It had been a while since I'd been under water. When I opened the doors, Jewel was sitting on the edge of the pool, flapping her tail in the water. She was holding a small turtle in her hand while feeding it seaweed. The pool room was like a forest and the water was pure. Different kinds of fish swam underneath and there were even a few octopuses in the pool.

"Come and sit. Show me your scales," she said.

I sat across from her in the pool, raised my shorts up, and stuck my legs into the water. Black, silver and gold scales covered my legs. Jewel's tail was somewhat similar, minus the silver.

"We have the same scales."

"What a coincidence," she said.

"I'm very thankful to you for allowing us to stay."

"Anytime, so tell me about yourself. Do you have a girlfriend?" she asked.

"I had one, but she passed away a few days before we came here."

"She was human?" she replied.

"Sorta, not really."

"Did you love her?" she asked.

"I cared for her until I saw the real her but that's old. I'm sorta feeling Rain, though. I mean we've gotten close in the past few days."

"So, tell me what you like about Rain?" she asked.

"I think she's beautiful."

"That's it?" she asked.

"There's more but I don't feel comfortable talking about it. I don't want you to get the wrong idea."

"I'm going to tell you a story. Once upon a time, there was a very beautiful fairy, but she wasn't like her other sisters. She was different because her looks weren't developed. She wasn't curvy or had big breasts like the others, but one day, she came across a creature that loved her for her heart. Weeks later, she went away to collect sea shells for her sisters. Sometimes she spent days collecting things to bring back to the reef for the ones she loved. But while she was gone, her lover looked for her. He came across one of her sisters and she was more beautiful than the one he once loved. He fell in love at first sight because she was shapely and had a beautiful mane. When the fairy came back with the seashells, she saw her lover and sister kissing and he chose the beautiful one. The beautiful sister wasn't aware her mate used to be with the ugly sister but when she found out, she apologized, but she didn't leave him alone. The beautiful sister got pregnant for her mate and he took her away from her reef sisters. She was miserable with him, she didn't want to get pregnant for him or spend her life with him, he was just something to do. She wanted to be free, but he held on to her knowing she didn't love him," she said.

"What's the point of your story?"

"If you don't see the point then maybe you deserve a broken heart. A beautiful face is enjoyable to look at, but a good heart is even better," she replied.

"So, what happened to the ugly one?"

"She turned into a beautiful fairy and that was her happy ending," she smirked.

"Your story doesn't make sense. Why didn't he get with the ugly sister after her looks changed since she's the one who really loved him? And what happened to the beautiful one?"

"I don't know. It's just one of those stories that leaves you hanging. But Reef likes you. I'm not taking any sides because I love them both but if you want something magical, go with the one your heart connects with instead of following your eyes and your male part," she said.

"Do you wanna smoke? I got the best kush in town."

"Don't be too sure," she laughed.

The door opened, and Shore walked in. I was trying to figure out why she wasn't at the lake. She left a few days ago and came right back. But I shrugged it off because it wasn't my business.

"When are you going home?" Jewel asked her.

"No time soon. My fish are gone."

"I'll let y'all two have girl-talk," I stated, getting up.

Reef was in the hallway when I left out of the pool room. She rolled her eyes at me and smacked her teeth. Reef was pretty, but she wasn't as beautiful as Rain. She was also too loud, had a foul mouth and she was a trouble maker.

"What's your problem today?" I asked.

"I want you to go home," she said.

"Why?"

"Because you and your father don't need to be the only men here twenty-four-seven. It's whack!" she said.

"I think you're just jealous because I like Rain."

"Shut up before I scratch your face, then nobody will want you!" she said.

"I'll just heal."

Reef flicked me off before she headed upstairs. I was on my way to check up on my father when a door in the hallway opened and someone pulled me in. It was Rain. We were in a small room with a lot of old dusty books, maybe it used to be an office. She was naked, looking more beautiful than ever. Rain pushed me down onto a chair and straddled me. I gripped her hips and she rubbed her pussy against my print. She was wet and warm.

"I want you to fuck me," she gritted against my ear, while her teeth scraped my neck. Rain's nipple was pressed against my lips. She was more experienced than me. I'd only been with one or two girls in that way. Rain knew it and it turned her on. She climbed off my lap and pulled my shorts down. My erection sprang free and she kissed the tip of it.

"Ohhh shitttttt," I groaned when she kissed the tip of my head. Rain's mouth stretched open while taking me to the back of her throat. My fingers got tangled in her hair while stroking her mouth. Rain's mouth was almost like pussy. The tip of her fingernails tickled my testicles, causing the blood flow to rush to the tip of my head. The veins in my dick widened as she took me in like an undertow. Rain hummed against my dick and pre-cum slipped from the head of my shaft. She moaned while tasting it.

"Give me some more, baby," she said between slurps. She used two hands, jerking me off while deep-throating me. I gripped her hair while slowly fucking her mouth. Her spit mixed with my sperm dripped down her chin after I exploded. Rain pulled away from me and wiped off her mouth, but I was still aroused. I got off the chair and picked her up, pressing her against the wall. She wrapped her legs around me while I eased my girth into her tight opening. Rain pulled my head down to her chest, so I could suck on her nipples.

"You're so big! You're in my stomach!" she screamed out when I hammered her into the wall. Her pussy muscles squeezed me, causing me to swell. Rain's body jerked and spasmed when the tip of my dick, pulsated against her G-spot. She screamed while her nails scratched at my neck and back. When I pressed further into her, she exploded on me. Rain choked me and told me to do it harder. The walls shook, and the ceiling cracked above us as I deeply fucked her. She threw her pussy back at me, matching my thrusts as she came. My nails left marks on her skin while busting inside of her. She fell into my chest and I kissed her forehead. What Jewel was saying kept creeping into my head. Rain was beautiful and had good sex, but we didn't talk about nothing. I pulled out of her and lowered her onto the floor.

"I'm going to take a shower," she said.

"Cool."

She grabbed her robe off the chair then opened the door; she peeked head out to make sure the coast was clear.

"I'll see you later," she said before leaving the room.

Three male water fairies were sitting in the foyer after I left the room. For the past few days, they'd just pop up with gifts and money for the girls. They were lames.

"Oh, look there goes the pool boy," one of them said but I kept walking. While I was going up the stairs, a bottle hit the back of my head. I tried to make peace inside Jewel's home since I was guest, so I kept quiet for the sake of Caspian's health, but they were pretty much punking me. I jumped down the spiral staircase.

"Which one of y'all threw that shit?" I asked.

"We don't know what you're talking about," one said.

"What are you going to do about it?" another one said. I grabbed him by the throat and slammed him onto the floor.

"Get off my brother!" one said while punching me. Two more male fairies walked down the hallway and into the foyer. I was surrounded by four of them.

"Your kind needs to stay with your kind! Leave our women alone!" someone said. My nails hooked into their brother's throat while I continued choking him. He turned into a water fairy, blue and silver scales covering his face. He spit some type of acid on me that burned my skin, but it didn't stop me.

"You're killing him!" they screamed. The brother scratched at my arms when I squeezed tighter. The four of them jumped on me, biting at my skin. I pulled away from their dying brother to fight them off. My nails and teeth ripped and tore at their flesh while they wrestled with me. Water exploded from my mouth, sending them sailing across the foyer. My wounds healed when I got up. They were badly wounded, but I wanted them dead. I picked up one and held him above my head. He kicked and screamed, begging me to let him ago while my mouth awaited his body to drop so I could bite him in half.

"Kill him if you want," Jewel said from behind me.

"NOOOOOOO! You're one of us! We have been bearing gifts all week! Please get this monster away from me!" the fairy said to Jewel."

"I heard your remarks, Dyan. You all have been poking the beast the past few days. So, I'm allowing him to kill you all. Learn to respect those who mind their business!" Jewel said.

I dropped Dyan's body into my mouth and snapped him in half. The other four jumped through the windows to get away and I chased after them. The water burst knocked them into the sand; the impact broke their spines. I ripped through them, dismembering their bodies while they were still halfway alive. The water from the ocean washed up on shore, pulling their body parts into the water. My body slowly changed into its human form, my locs disappearing, the scales sinking underneath my skin. My stomach rumbled, and my throat swelled. I fell into the sand and hurled up chewed-up flesh and bones. Jewel came outside and put a blanket around me.

"You're shedding," she said while peeling old skin off my face.

"From my wounds healing."

"More so because you're growing. You look a half inch taller," she said. The water fairies ran outside seconds later.

"What happened? Why is the foyer ruined and what was that loud noise?" Darya asked.

"Oh, nothing, I let a deer run loose in the house and Bay chased it," Jewel said.

"Our dates were supposed to pick us up and there is blood everywhere!" Lake said.

"Bay is shedding so he bleeds. Now, let's clean up," Jewel said, dismissing them.

"That was a horrible lie."

"That's because I'm not much of a liar. Now, go get cleaned up so you can fix my windows. I told you to kill them, not mess up my house!" she said, walking away. I relaxed on the sand for a while. It felt good to be out of the house. I saw a silhouette out of the corner of my eye coming towards me. When it closer, I realized it was Shore. She sat next to me and crossed her legs. Shore was the most beautiful one of all, but she was taken. Her attitude was easy to deal with but there was a cattiness to her. She pushed her green curls behind her ear and that's when I noticed her tears.

"What's up with you?"

"I miss Zambezi," she said.

"Well, go to him, then. It's not right for you to be here while your sisters entertain those men. You're taken."

"I know but I don't care about them. I'm sad because I know I was the reason behind us breaking up. My locket shows me things that have been giving me second thoughts about everything," she said.

"Can it show you if he cheated or not?"

"I tried but nothing came up. I think because the woman isn't a part of the waters, she just pretends to be. Sorta like your mother," Shore said.

"I'm not just saying this because that's big bro, but I can't see him doing it. Maybe if you were his ex-girlfriend but not you. His life was beginning to evolve around yours and that's unusual for him because he never lets anyone get between him and his goals. I think you're trippin' and listening to your single sisters. Go home, Shore."

"I am. Now, go take a shower. You smell like sex and old blood," she playfully gagged.

"I'm going to remember that the next time you and Zam sneak off and come back smelling like dolphin ass," I said, getting up.

"Bye-bye now!" she waved me off.

I went into the house and headed upstairs to my father's bedroom. He was standing in the window, looking out at the waves.

"You're finally out of bed."

"It took me a long time to stand up, almost felt my knees crack, but don't worry yourself. We'll be out of here soon. I know those damn fairies are a headache," he said.

"I don't get it, Father. The fairies have been very nice to you, but you keep discrediting them. What have they done to you? You thought my mother was one of them and Zambezi's mother is one, too. What's up with that?"

He turned around and faced me. Me and my brother were the spitting image of our father. We had his height, complexion and build. We even had the same exact hair type as him, but we didn't have his heart. At one point, Zambezi had our father's ways until Shore came along.

"They won't ever love you. Maybe Shore is different than them, so I'll count her out. She was raised differently but the ones that spend time in the waters, aren't worth a sea stone. You're better off with a human girl like the one back in Oland. I know you have a thing for one of them," he said.

"Ara isn't human anymore. Mother changed her into something like she did the others in town."

"My market is in shambles and it's Zambezi's fault," he said.

That's all my father ever cared about, his market. Zambezi thought I was his favorite, but it was far from the truth; I was my mother's favorite. I had a detachment with my father. Now that he was better, his ways of thinking were back to normal.

"Stay away from that bitch, Jewel. She's nothing but trouble," he said.

I heard great things about my father and his clan from many years ago. My father was one of the leaders because he helped create the waters by causing rain, and the fairies nourished in it. Together, they were all like a family, but something happened along the way.

"I'm a man now. You can't tell me what to do. I'm not moving back with you when we return to Oland."

He sat on the bed with his back facing me as his shoulders sank. "I've been thinking about going to the Caribbean Sea to build a small house on an island. I have nothing here anymore. You and your brother are grown now. When I hatched from an egg, my parents weren't around. Come to find out, the Earth gave birth to me, along with the fairies. Even though we were born that way, we're still able to give life, but some of us don't know how to be something we never had. All I know is the waters. I thought moving on land and living my life as a human would've changed my mindset, but it made it worse because I put my life into the market instead of my sons. You should've let me die," he said.

I had nothing to say to my father because he gave up a long time ago and I gave up on him myself. I wanted him to live but I wouldn't miss him if he never came back to Oland; maybe it was for the better. I left his bedroom and went to the shower room in the hallway. While in the shower, I thought of my mother. I wondered if she was okay and hoped someone was watching over her. My father and brother wanted me to stay away from Adwoa, but she was still my mother.

*Maybe Jewel can help her the same way she helped my father.*

# Shore

**The next day...**

The cabin was empty when I arrived home. Zambezi's scent still lingered through the cabin. I was alone, my mother was away, and Zambezi had left. Even my fish were gone. The kitchen table was ruined, and the chairs were broken up from the fight. I had enough money saved up from what my mother left me and what Zambezi was paying me from the market. As much as I loved the lake, my life was less complicated when I didn't have this locket and lived in the hood with the regular humans. Someone walked into my cabin while I was sweeping.

"What happened?" Reef asked.

"I thought you were staying back?"

"I followed you. We never let you leave our house alone. Someone always follows you and it was my turn. I just wanted to come in because I didn't have a reason to rush back home," she said.

"You all don't have to do that for me. This little locket packs a punch."

"It can't see from behind, but anyways, let's go into town," Reef said.

"I'm not in the mood to be around anyone right now."

"Bitch, if you don't snap out of it! Zambezi isn't going anywhere, trust me. But why are you here and not looking for him if you want him back?" she asked.

"What do I say?"

"How about sucking his dick for starters," Reef said.

Reef was very blunt, so blunt it made me cringe sometimes. She said whatever she wanted to, even if it hurt your feelings.

"You're only nineteen! What in the hell are you even saying? Have you ever been in love? And, plus, I doubt if Zambezi can fit in my mouth."

"I don't have to be in love to know the way to a man's heart. Just suck him off really good and he'll forget what happened. That's what Lake taught us anyway," Reef said, and I rolled my eyes.

"I'm so not listening to you right now. You know what I want to do? I want to visit my old neighborhood, but we don't have a car."

"Where the human men have those gold things in their mouths and some of them sell that white dust-looking stuff?" she asked.

"Not all of them were drug dealers and it's cocaine."

"Did you have a lake or something in your old neighborhood?" she asked.

"Nope, just a pool," I said, and she cringed.

"Ewww, I'm disgusted. How about you find Zambezi while I stay here. We can be roommates," she said.

"Wait, you're moving in?"

*Why is everyone moving into my damn cabin?*

"Okay, fine, I hate being around Rain and Bay. I just don't get it. He's my age and she's never messed around with someone his age! It's like she didn't want him until I told her how sexy he is. She only wanted him for sex in the beginning and now they're sneaking off and fucking everywhere! I'm sick of hearing her moans when I walk down the hallway. They think I don't know they sneak into the office room," she said.

"He chose Rain, and it's hard to swallow, but you have to accept it."

"I am I just don't want to see it. So, in the meantime, where is my bedroom?" Reef asked, and I pointed to my mother's room. Reef went into the bedroom while I finished cleaning up. Afterwards, I was exhausted. I went into my room and laid across my bed. The scent from Zambezi's hair was on the pillow next to me. I snuggled against it and my eyes got heavy. It wasn't easy sleeping in Jewel's house because it was always busy and noisy, plus I had gotten used to sleeping next to Zambezi. Suddenly, I closed my eyes and welcomed sleep…

*"You can't have that baby, Oceana. I'll kill you if you don't get rid of it," a man said.*

*"You lay a finger on me and I'll make you disappear! I thought you loved me and now you want me to just get rid of something? My kind doesn't believe in this, what do you want me to do? Stab myself in the womb?" Oceana asked.*

*"I'm not what you think I am. I seduced you because my mother told me to. Please don't have that baby. It'll shame my kind, Oceana," he said.*

*"What are you talking about, Tahoe? I am your kind! We're from the waters!" Oceana shouted.*

*They were inside a forest, underneath the waterfall. The man had his back towards Oceana as she sat on a rock and cried. I reached out to her, but my fingers went through her.*

"I'm not what you think I am. Although I look like your kind, I turn into something else, something wicked. If she's a cross between our worlds, she might have to choose a side," he said.

"She'll have my spirit, I can feel her, but I know you're something else because my locket doesn't show you, but I fell in love with you anyway. You're not wicked, Tahoe. Tell me what it is so I can help you," Oceana said.

"I'll be punished if I tell you. I was only supposed to get close to you to steal your locket. I didn't think you were going to be with child, Oceana," he said.

"I'm going to spare your life because I know you're just talking to push me away. If you were wicked, you wouldn't be telling me this secret of yours," Oceana said. She slid off the rock and went to him. He dropped his head and wept while Oceana comforted him. Tahoe pulled out a machete and I yelled for Oceana to get away. She couldn't see it because his back was towards her.

"GET AWAY!" I yelled.

*Tahoe pulled away from Oceana and fear settled in her eyes when he turned around. He swung his machete at her and it cut across her stomach. She fell onto the ground, holding her stomach. I ran to her and tried to shield her, but I fell through her.*

*"I loved you, too, Oceana, but I can't let them know I gave you a child," Tahoe said. He brought the machete down to cut her head off, but the locket opened and turned him to dust. Oceana fell onto the ground and sobbed for her lover...*

"SHORE, WAKE UP!" Reef screamed while shaking me. I woke up and the bed was soaking wet.

"You were screaming in your sleep and your locket flooded your cabin," Reef said. When I sat up, I saw that the water was up to Reef's knees while things floated around.

"I had a dream about my father. I think he was one of Adwoa's children. Why wouldn't Jewel or Giva tell me my father was one of those things? I don't look like them."

"Dreams or visions from your locket? Dreams aren't real," Reef said.

"You're right. It just seemed so real. I would look like a creature if it was true. I've been having the weirdest dreams since I was a kid."

"Didn't you say a woman came to Zambezi about Adwoa? Where is she? Maybe that's why you had the dream," Reef asked.

"I don't know where she is."

"Maybe Zambezi knows. Let's find him," Reef said.

I don't know how it came to mind but sometimes it seemed as if the locket spoke to me. The flood in the cabin disappeared after I dipped my locket into the water. Everything inside was back to normal.

"You're so lucky to have one of those," Reef said.

"I wish I didn't. My mother needs to come back, so she can take it back."

"Have you tried to look for her in the locket?" Reef replied.

"No, I'm afraid to. What if she's still an alcoholic? I wouldn't be able to live with myself if I find out she lied to me. She said she's coming back and I'm taking her word. But enough about me, let's go find Zambezi."

Reef left out of my bedroom and I went into the kitchen to grab a key. Afterwards, I went inside my bedroom to get dressed. It was scorching hot out, so I settled for a tank top and shorts with a pair of tennis shoes. While looking in the mirror, I brushed my hair into a bushy ponytail. Reef came into my room seconds later, wearing a half top and wrap-around skirt. She took my lip gloss off my dresser then applied it to her lips.

"I don't know where your mouth been. Plus, where we are going, you won't feel pretty at all," I said.

"Stop hating, now let's go," she replied. Reef pulled me out my bedroom and out of the cabin. My nerves were spinning out of control because I didn't know what to say to Zambezi once I found him.

# Zambezi

*B*e patient, big boy. It's coming! I told my dragon.

I was waiting in the water, as four deer drank from the river. While my stomach was growling, my body changed, camouflaging with the water. The tail of my dragon had a sharp clasp at the end. Sometimes I used it to catch more than one deer. Slowly swimming up towards the surface, I was careful not to cause waves strong enough to scare them away.

*1...2...3!*

My snout pierced through the surface, snatching two deer into the mouth of my monster. One of them ran away but I caught the third one, the sharp clasp at the end of my tail pierced through the deer's neck and snatched him into the river. I took my food underneath, crushing through the bones of my meal. Blood and animal particles floated around me while the teeth of my dragon shredded the deer, so it was easy to swallow. Once he was finished eating, my body turned back to human form. I swam to the land nearby and rested against a tree to sunbathe. For the past three days, I'd been staying out in the waters. Being away from Shore was driving me crazy. One second, I felt relieved of her and the next I craved the warmth of her body next to mine.

*Stop thinking about Shore! Fuck her!* I thought as I got dressed in shorts, a T-shirt and tennis shoes. It was time for me to go to the market. I reached into the pocket of my shorts for my car key. My boat was at the bottom of Lake Deep, broken up so it took me more time to drive into the city. By the time I made it to the fish market, I only had an hour to set up. When I unlocked the door, everything was put out.

"BAY!" I called out. He was the only one besides me who had a key. I heard noises coming from the back along with giggles. A familiar scent breezed past me while getting closer to the back. Shore came out of the back room wearing a rubber apron and gloves and Reef came out behind her.

"Good morning, I hope you don't mind our help," Shore said.

"Well, actually I need to get paid for this," Reef said.

"Why do you have lemons on ice?" I asked Reef.

"Isn't this how humans make lemonade?" she asked. She rolled her eyes and went back into the freezer room. Shore couldn't look at me, her attention was on the tray of fresh salmon.

"So, what, you just gonna stand there and not say shit?"

"I'm sorry for reacting the way I did but I'm not apologizing for fighting that creature you had in my cabin. She's from Adwoa's clan so therefore, she's the enemy despite her wanting to switch sides," Shore said. After spending three days thinking about everything that happened, I wasn't really mad that she stayed out because of my father. At first, I was hot, but it was selfish of me to overreact. Shore attacking me was something I couldn't get out of my head. Even though I healed from her wounds, I wanted to kill her at that time because she was triggering my inner-being.

"I apologize, too, but you put your hands on me without hearing me out. I'm not into that. I wanted to snap your neck and bite the shit out of you. You were trying to kill me. That's a problem because that means if anything goes bad between us, you'll attack me. So, what do you have to say about that?"

"I already apologized," she said.

"Yeah, I heard it, but that's all you gonna say?"

"I won't put my hands on you anymore, but you know I can't control it sometimes," she said.

"We're done the next time you do that again so tell that crazy thing inside of you that a beautiful face can't save her anymore."

I walked over to Shore and took the tray out of her hand. She leaned against my chest and I wrapped an arm around her, bending down to kiss her lips.

"I missed you," she said while I kept kissing her.

"I missed you more. How did you get in?" I asked, pulling away from her.

"Well, Bay leaves the key on the counter, so I took it," she replied.

"I quit," Reef said when she came out the back.

"Already?" Shore asked.

"I'll be outside smoking. This is a death house. How are you okay with him killing our fish? This is sooo wrong," Reef said.

"Why you still standing here if you quit? Peace out!" I said.

Reef smacked her teeth and mumbled under her breath while walking to the back.

"Out of all of your sister-friends, you had to bring that one? She's mad annoying." Shore elbowed me and told me to be quiet before she heard me.

"Where have you been staying?" she asked, dumping ice on the shrimp.

"I've been living in a river. It's relaxing sometimes, it makes you feel less human because your feelings aren't everywhere. What about you?"

"I've been at Jewel's until this morning. Your father is getting better. He's even walking around his room now," she said.

"That's what's up. Thank you for that. What's up with Bay? He acts like he doesn't have a brother or something."

"He's coming back soon. He told me that before I left," she replied.


Since most of the stuff was already done, I turned on the, *Open,* sign. There were a few cars parked on side of the road, waiting to see the market open. I told Shore to keep Reef in the back, so she wouldn't mess up my business. The door opened ten minutes after I turned on the sign. Around eight dudes walked in. One of them was a familiar face. It was the dread-head dude that wanted Shore.

"I have a message for your little brother. Tell him I know he killed my brothers and I'm going to see that I drain every drop of blood from his body!" the dread-head shouted.

"Go home, Nerida. We don't know what you're talking about," Shore said.

"I can give you the world. All you have to do is leave this poor trash alone. That car he got outside, I have three of them. My bedroom is bigger than this shithole. By the way, I want to see you in that short dress again," he said.

"Yo, just go home and we can talk about this later. This is stupid, and nobody is touching my little brother, so that's dead."

"Oh, you think you're untouchable? My brothers went to Jewel's house and never came back. A little birdie told me your brother ate them. Your kind ain't shit but nasty bottom feeders!" Nerida replied.

"Bruh, you sound like a bitch and your brothers look like goddesses. Tell me something, bro. How does it feel to have a glowing tail with colorful fish scales? You think I'm afraid of a male fairy? What color is your hair when you turn? Be honest. I bet it's pink with purple highlights. Y'all are a joke to me," I said while wrapping my arm around Shore's hip. Nerida was jealous, he wanted something he couldn't have. I was an alpha male of my kind and he was one of his kind. He came into my place of business with his brothers, so he could feel more superior and hopefully win over Shore.

"You can make all the jokes you want but your mate will be mine. I always get what I want," Nerida said. I felt myself changing but I knew a human or two was going to walk through the doors.

"We can talk about this later."

"Sure, we can," Nerida said.

On his way out the door, he knocked over the shrimp counter.

"So, why you ain't tell me his bitch-ass was around you at Jewel's house? What kind of dress he talking about? See why I keep getting pissed off?" I asked. Shore ignored me while she was cleaning up the floor.

"You deaf?"

"Can you just stop being a jackass for a minute? We left that in the past! But to answer your question, yes, he was there, and I did have on something revealing but that's because I couldn't fit a lot of their clothes! Did I touch anyone, NO! Did anyone touch me? NO! The answer is NO to all of your questions!" she said while slamming the shrimp in a bucket.

"I asked you a few days ago if your sister was trying to get you to talk to someone else and you didn't answer me. So, is it Nerida they are trying to hook you up with? At least tell me because the muthafucka keeps coming here like he's entitled to you."

"Lake was trying to persuade her into talking to Nerida because he's rich and, well, you come from a small poor town like Oland," Reef said from behind me.

"Do you ever mind your damn business?" Shore asked Reef.

"Well, the conversation is open for a third person. I mean y'all should've whispered if I wasn't supposed to know. Plus, I was in the back watching and waiting for the fight," Reef shrugged.

I headed to the back to change my shoes and Shore followed me.

"I don't want him," she said.

"I know that. I'm gonna kill him, though, and I don't want to hear nothing about it. Matter of fact, I got something else for him. I knew I disliked his wanna-be-gangster preppy ass for a reason."

Shore sat on my lap and rested on my shoulder. While she was quiet, I could hear her thoughts. She was blaming herself for Nerida's actions.

"Promise me we'll always be together," she said.

"I think we're stuck together."

"Okay, now let's get to work. I heard someone come in," Shore said. She climbed off my lap and her backside jiggled. I reached out to grab her ass and she smacked my hand away.

"It's like that now?"

"First it starts off with you touching my butt then it'll end up with moaning and groaning," she said.

"You got a point."

We walked out the back and Reef was taking orders. She was friendly, and the sound of her voice was innocent.

"Reef is a lunatic," Shore laughed.

"This is going to be a long day."

"Let's get busy, big boy," Shore said while heading to the register.

Shore didn't have to do as much as she did for the market, but she enjoyed doing it. One day I asked her why she overworked herself and her answer was that she always wanted to work but she had an illness. Despite the evil side to her, she was perfect.

*Should I tell her I fell in love with her or should I wait? Yeah, I'll wait so that way she won't think we're moving too fast.*

"Can you grab me some more plastic bags?" Reef asked.

"No problem."

It was a human's holiday, July 4th, and it was very busy. I was somewhat appreciative that Reef helped out because it would've been too hectic if I was by myself.

## Seven hours later...

The seafood was gone, and the market was closed. I counted the money while Shore and Reef mopped the floor and, of course, Reef couldn't keep her mouth shut.

"My arms are tired," Reef said.

"Welcome to the working life where you don't have to depend on a man to take care of you.

Maybe Jewel should make all of y'all work instead of fucking those bitch-ass fairy boys."

"ZAMBEZI!" Shore said.

"What? You want me to pretend like Jewel's mansion isn't a whore house?"

"We're not whores! We just love the finer things in life and watch your mouth before I snatch your tongue out," Reef said.

"Okay, how about I reword it? Y'all deserve better than to let them use you for your looks. Gifts and money shouldn't make you fall for the trap. They see y'all as whores. I'm just looking out for y'all even though I could care less."

"I'm still a virgin!" Reef said. She slammed her mop on the floor and stormed to the back.

*No way Reef is a virgin.*

I went to the back to see what was up with Reef and she was sitting on a cooler crying. Shore came to the back and sat next to her. Reef was sobbing, screaming like someone was killing her.

*This is the bull I'm talking about. Overdramatic for no reason! All that mouth she has, and she wants to cry about nothing.*

"What's the matter?" Shore asked.

"I pretend to be fast because it attracts the boys. Lake told me to fake it until I made it. She's the one who has the parties and introduces us to the men, Jewel just lets us. But Bay thought I was going to give it up to him because I came on to him too strong. He turned to Rain when I told him I was a virgin. He also said Zambezi told him to never get involved with a virgin because they're crazy," Reef said.

"You didn't have to say all that, damn. Dry snitching for nothing," I said.

"You really told Bay that?" Shore asked while Reef smiled at me.

"Look at her! She's faking it," I said. Shore looked at Reef and she was looking sad all over again.

"Oh, I see what you're doing. And, yeah, I told Bay that. He's still a teenager and he doesn't need to deal with it, not with Reef anyway. She's childish."

"I'm not crazy," Shore said in confusion.

"Y'all ready to leave? I need to eat," I said, changing the subject.

I left them in the back to have girl-talk while I locked everything up. By the time we got outside, the sun was going down. It was the longest time I spent at the market, usually I could catch the sun.

"I could go for a swim right now," Shore said, walking towards my car. I unlocked the doors and Reef got into the back seat.

"This area has a lot of humans around this time of the year. You'll be taking a risk," I said, getting in.

"So, you bought this with fish market money?" Reef asked about my car.

"Naw, I was a pimp. Why does it matter to you anyway?"

"I'm just asking! Stop being a dickhead," she said.

"Shore, get your reef sister or whatever the hell she is before I scale her. She talking too much."

"Fish markets bring in a lot of money, Reef. Humans are big seafood eaters and even chefs come to the markets to get it wholesale. Don't sleep on it," Shore said.

"That's all he had to say," Reef said.

"You saw how many people was in there today? What in the hell I need to explain for, fish brain? You're definitely not smarter than a clam."

"That's why you're going to be a daddy," Reef said, and I almost swerved off the road.

"You're pregnant?" I asked Shore and she blushed.

"No, Reef is just teasing you, but why do you look upset?" Shore asked.

"Because he doesn't want to father your child," Reef said.

"Enough, Reef! You're always messing with him, leave him alone!" Shore yelled at her. Reef sat back in the seat and crossed her arms.

*Finally, the brat is silent!*

The rest of the way towards Oland was quiet. Reef was sleep and Shore was playing in her hair. She was thinking about the conversation we had moments prior.

*Why would he be upset if I was pregnant? I don't want to be a mother neither, but we have something special, what's wrong if something good came out of that? Maybe I shouldn't think about this, okay, never mind. I have to think about this since we're intimate. Maybe Zambezi would follow his father's footsteps and be a horrible father,* Shore thought.

Honestly, I was in my feelings since she kept comparing me to my father. Maybe she saw something in me that I couldn't for her to think that way. When I glanced over at Shore, she looked worried, but I kept quiet. I had two choices: prove to her that I wasn't like him or leave since I'd been wanting to leave Oland for years. Shore was thinking about a baby, something I wasn't ready for her and neither was she. I was so caught up with being inside her, I wasn't thinking about the outcome. Now I was worried if she was really pregnant or not.

# Shore

I woke up to Zambezi carrying me in his arms. Reef was walking behind us while we were going through the woods.

"You fell asleep during the ride and I didn't want to wake you," Zambezi said. I stretched my arms and legs while yawning. Zambezi stood me up after I told him I was fine enough to walk on my own. Reef was smoking and taking a drink out of her canteen. There was someone sitting in front of the cabin once we came out of the woods. She stood up when I approached her; it was the girl Zambezi saved. I never got a good look at her face when we got into a fight, but she was gorgeous. Her long braids hung past her shoulders and the dress she wore clung to her slim but curvy body. *What man can resist her?* I thought.

"I've been waiting here since the sun was up. I want to speak with you," she said to me.

"Is that the bitch you caught naked in your cabin? I don't know, Shore. She's pretty damn sexy. You think they didn't do anything when he got drunk? You said there was an empty liquor bottle in front of him when you came home," Reef whispered in my ear. I ignored her because I promised Zambezi I'd trust him, but there was still that small voice in the back of my mind asking me, "what if?"

"Say what you have to say then leave my fucking property!" I shouted at the girl.

"Yo, relax," Zambezi said.

"Mind your business!"

That voice inside my head was telling me to attack those around me.

*NOT NOW! Let's hear what she has to say!*

*Or you can kill her. She wants your mate. She's seducing him with her body. She craves his blood! She's the enemy and you have to kill to be happy again. Or you can cut off his dick and feed it to the crabs. Do what you must!* The other side of me said. My nails were sprouting out, curving into fish hooks.

"She's one of us," the girl said.

"What are you talking about, Lesidi?" Zambezi asked.

"I saw it when she attacked me. She's a sea demon, too," Lesidi said. I grabbed her by the throat and lifted her body off the ground. She was kicking and telling me to stop.

"I can help you!" she gasped.

"You want to kill me and take what's mine! I don't need your help!" Lesidi sent a bone crushing kick to my throat and I dropped her. She ran behind Zambezi and it angered me. Reef placed her hand on my shoulder and I pushed her away from me. My feet transformed into fins but I wanted to stop it before I hurt Zambezi and Reef. I dug my nails into my neck. All I could think about was the dream I had about my parents which I thought wasn't real. Blood poured from my neck and Zambezi rushed to me. He pried my fingers away, so I could heal but I didn't want to.

"I don't want this inside of me! Get it out!" I yelled. Lesidi kneeled next to me while Zambezi rocked me.

"You have to live with it, but it'll feed off your anger. If you can calm down, it'll go away," Lesidi said.

"Get away from her!" Reef said to Lesidi.

"Your hate shouldn't be against me," Lesidi said.

"Well, too bad because it is! Your kind attacked Shore. They want her locket. How do we know this isn't a setup? Maybe Shore isn't one of you. She's too beautiful to be an ugly creature," Reef said.

"She might not look like us, but she can be ugly on the inside. We can be just like you as long as we use the sea dragon's blood. Beauty comes and goes, nothing stays beautiful forever," Lesidi said.

"We do!" Reef said.

"But you fairies have ugly ways that you wear on your face," Lesidi replied.

"Not as ugly as the shark-looking creature you turn into," Reef said. While they were arguing, I held Shore in my arms. She was scared, and I wanted to take it all away.

"Go home, Lesidi," I replied.

# Zambezi

"**Y**ou want to ignore this? If she keeps getting angry, she'll kill us all! Breeds of water fairies and sea demons are a bad mix. They don't pick a side, they'll go against both instead. Since she has the locket, she's more of a threat to all of us!" Shore pulled away from me and went inside the cabin and we followed.

"Where is Adwoa?" Shore asked Lesidi.

"I don't want you all to get hurt! There are many, many sea demons in the swamp, some even hide in the mud. It's more than the ones who come from Oland, some are there from centuries ago. I'm talking hundreds," Lesidi said.

"The locket will kill them," Shore said.

"Most of those people were tricked into Adwoa's beliefs. They don't deserve cruel punishment," Lesidi said.

"They deserve to die!" Reef said.

"If we all need death then so does Shore. Are you saying your kind is worthier?" Lesidi asked Reef.

"Yes, we are because Earth gave us life. Can you say the same for yourself?" Reef asked.

"I was born from a human, so yes I can," Lesidi replied.

"But your kind still isn't a water spirit, so the waters didn't birth you!" Reef said.

"All water people are water spirits and that includes me. I'm just not what you are but it doesn't make me any different. Am I not supposed to be welcomed into the waters because of my looks?" Lesidi replied.

"Of course, you're not welcomed. Why fuck up beautiful waters with creatures that look like plankton?" Reef asked.

"Because of your reef sister's mouth, I'll be at Zambezi's property when you're ready to talk," Lesidi said to Shore.

"You live in his house?" Shore asked.

"It's Adwoa's old cabin. I don't have no place else to go," Lesidi while leaving out of the cabin.

"Do not listen to her, Shore. You're not one of them. She wants you to be her friend, so she can steal your locket. My mother told me that we're hated amongst other water spirits and they'll do anything to destroy us. Please don't fall for it. So what you get angry, we all do," Reef said. She kissed Shore on the forehead before going into the other room.

"Lesidi just doesn't seem sincere. Maybe it's a part of what she is but I don't trust her. My feelings still haven't changed. I don't want her around us. If I was one of them, I'd know which god Adwoa worships and perhaps know how to find her," Shore said. She went inside the bedroom and took her clothes off for the shower, and just like that she was back to normal. I didn't know who to believe: Lesidi or Shore. Maybe she was one of them or maybe she wasn't, but time would tell soon. She grabbed my things for the shower and told me to join her. I went outside to the back of the cabin where the shower was located. Shore turned the knob on the shower pole while I undressed. Once I stepped into the shower with her, she wrapped her arms around me. Shore was aroused. I felt the heat from her center against my leg. She stroked my erection while I caressed her breasts. Her eyes turned blue with a green tint, almost the same as her hair. Scales appeared on her chest, glowing against my skin. Looking at her beauty, it was hard to believe something like a sea demon was inside her. She placed my hand between her legs and she was soaking wet. Her clit swelled while I rubbed her mound. She leaned against the wooden wall of the shower and wrapped one leg around me. My finger entered her while thumbing her clit. Shore pulled away from the wall while I was finger-fucking her. Her walls kissed my finger as it squeezed around it. Her nipples hardened, and I took one into my mouth, gently sinking my teeth into her flesh. Shore rocked her hips, getting into rhythm as my finger stroked her. Her lips turned gold, the shimmery lips were of her water fairy. My dick swelled, ready to penetrate. I removed my finger and turned her around, so her face could be against the wall. Her ass jiggled as I squeezed her cheeks. Shore's ass was soft like cotton. I grabbed a fist full of her hair and pulled it a little while my other hand was around her throat. With her head back, I was able to kiss her neck. She moaned while her nails clawed at the wall. Shore arched her back when my dick bumped against the center.

"How do you want me to make love to you, beautiful?"

"I want you to handle me, baby," she said, making my dick harder. Shore hissed when I teased her between her slit by pressing my head against her entrance then taking it away to rub against her slit. Warm essence from her dripped onto my shaft. My dick was pulsating, causing the head to swell. The veins were throbbing loudly. Shore jumped when the tip squeezed through her tunnel. Looking down while watching my dick spread her ass apart from entering, reminded me of a submarine, sailing through two large rocks. I turned the shower off, so I could only feel her wetness. Shore's essence saturated me while gliding through her walls.

"Play with your clit, beautiful," I coached her. She reached down and touched herself while I was pulsating—vibrating inside of her. Her legs trembled, and her pants grew louder. I gripped both of her cheeks and pushed further into her, hitting the spot that made her essence thicken like honey. Scales covered her back, traveling upwards around her neck. With each stroke, they glowed. It happened whenever I reached her G-spot.

"BABBYYYYYY!" she cried while I slammed into her. Her juices splashed onto my pelvis as she came.

"Throw it back, Shore! I wanna see that wave," I groaned, pounding into her warm flesh. I knew she couldn't throw it back yet because my size filled her, but it turned me on whenever she tried. Her ass cheeks jiggled from the vibration. She was sliding, almost to the floor so I turned her around and picked her up. With her legs tightly wrapped around me. I lowered her onto my erection. Her nails scratched my back while pushing upwards. She closed her eyes and threw her head back when I slid her up and down my shaft. Shore was able to work her hips in that position. She bucked her hips forward and I pumped into her. She was on the verge of exploding. Once Shore's whole body was covered in scales, even her face, I knew she was going to have an orgasmic wave. Her walls gripped me firmer than before and the vibration from me bounced off her walls and gave me the same feeling. I lowered myself on the floor while still holding her, so my knees wouldn't buckle. Shore's moans were loud enough to be heard from a mile away. She was speaking in a different language and I didn't know what she was saying but it was making me swell again. I gripped her hips to bury myself inside of her.

"I'm CUMMMMMMMINGGGGG!" Shore cried out while her body twitched.

"ARRRRGHHHHHHH!" I exploded, forgetting to pull out.

She fell into me and I wrapped my arms around her while she kissed me.

"You think Reef heard us?" she asked, licking my lips.

"You care?"

"Yes, this is personal," she said, followed by a moan. I was hard again and ready for another round and she was, too. Once we started, it took us hours to stop. Shore was addictive, and just as the saying goes, "Maybe it's something in the water."

# Adwoa

**Four days later...**

It was night time and the swamp smelled of death. A lot of my children died from the curse. I stood on the deck of the ship, overlooking the swamp. Many of my children were burying their siblings in the mushy mud. My lover wrapped his arms around me and kissed the back of my neck.

"I've failed Elonora."

"All we need is us. We can move to another small town and start over," he said.

"It's not that simple! I'm getting weak. I've never had to hide for this long. I don't have the fight in me, so I want you to take the ones who are still strong with you and kill Shore. I've waited long enough, and the clock is ticking."

"But we already have something special of hers," he said.

"That doesn't help me! Do what I said, make yourself useful!" He pulled away from me and went back inside the ship. I felt my face and it had wrinkles. A tear fell from eye. I felt a slight breeze and the night got quiet. Usually I heard the snakes and insects making noises after the sun went down. A shadow appeared next to me. I hadn't seen or heard her in many years. Elonora looked more than beautiful since the last time I saw her. Her bouncy burnt-orange hair smelled of sea salt with a scent of flowers. She wore a gold wrap-around dress and her scales were the color of the sky during the day. She also had orange sparkling lips that shined like diamonds.

"My child, my child. What have you done? I had to leave my kingdom for this?" she asked.

"I'm too weak and Caspian is gone. What else can I do to keep from aging?"

"I told you what to do. What is this, Adwoa? Look at your kingdom!" she said with her face twisted in disgust.

"I think you tricked me, Elonora. You sent me here and I don't know what to do."

"Ohhh, yes you do. I want this world to be like us and I want the locket. That locket belongs to me and you and your children will get it for me. I don't care about the princess or her mother! I want my locket! None of my children have gotten as far as you, Adwoa. I want you to keep going because with that locket, I won't have to turn to this thing and I can return to the waters where I came from! For many years I've haunted the lost ships that sailed through the swamp areas. My time will come," she said.

"And what happens to us?"

"I'll turn you all to the water fairies you're meant to be. This is the moment I've been waiting for. I knew that locket was going to resurface once Oceana and her sisters reunited. All you have to do is get it from around Shore's neck. Stop worrying about the sea dragon's blood, it was only a temporary fix since the locket was lost. Trust my word, Adwoa. You've came so far and you're so close. If I have to get the locket myself, that makes you all useful," she said. Elonora gave me a black pearl before disappearing. Jordan, one of my sons, came onto the ship's deck.

"You have someone here to see you," he said.

"I don't accept visitors! Who is it?" I asked.

"A man that wants a favor," he said.

I walked down the stairs to get to the main level of the ship. A few unfamiliar faces were in my presence.

"What do you want? And how did you find me?" I asked them.

"One of your children is dating my brother but that's not important. I'm here because I want something. I heard you grant wishes," the stranger said.

"But I must have something in return. What will you offer me?" I asked.

"Someone told me you want this special locket and I'll help you get it, but there are two sea dragons I want dead. My kind can't defeat them on their own. It will have to take my brothers and your children to kill them," he said.

"Tell me more."

"One of the brothers is at an elder water fairy's mansion by the name of Jewel. Her mansion is on a secluded beach far away from here.  Help me kill him and I'll get you the locket," he said.

"What's their names?"

"Zambezi and Bay," he said.

"What else did my child tell your brother?"

"That's all, why does it matter?" he asked.

"It doesn't matter at all. Your wish just might be granted."

*The stupid fairy doesn't know Bay is my son, so I can use him to my advantage. Then afterwards, I'm going to kill him.*

# Shore

**The next day...**

"Shore, wake up. It's time for me to return home. I'm just letting you know, I'm leaving," Reef said. I was taking a nap on the rock by the lake when she woke me up. It was getting late and I was still exhausted after helping Zambezi at the market hours prior.

"Okay, I'm up."

Zambezi was in the back of the cabin fixing it up. All I heard was loud banging and a chain saw. I climbed off the rock to let Zambezi know I was leaving to make sure Reef made it home safely. When I walked to the back of the cabin, Zambezi was shirtless and hacking wood.

"I'm going to make sure Reef makes it home."

"Hold on, I'll go with you. It's time for me to see my father and brother," he said. He picked up the log and sat it in the pile. The tree logs were heavy, and Zambezi carried it without breaking a sweat.

"It would've taken ten human men to carry that."

"Your man is special," he smirked.

"My man, huh?"

"You already know," he replied.


He picked me up and tossed me over his shoulder. "Put me down!" I hollered. Zambezi ran towards the lake as my head bounced off his back. He dived in, and our bodies transformed. My tail wrapped around him, pulling him closer to me. He wrapped his arms around me then kissed me.


*Hellloooo, I'm down here! Can we go now?* Reef thought. She swam underneath us. I pulled away from Zambezi and followed Reef. Zambezi's long body glided on top of mine. Whenever we were underwater, he swam on top of me, to protect me. I twisted my body around, so I could face him. A school of fish surrounded us while we kissed. I couldn't get enough of him. His glowing green eyes bored into mine. I noticed Zambezi's eyes changed in the water; sometimes they were a blueish-green and often times they were ocean blue. If I had to describe Zambezi to someone, I'd compare him to the blue tall people in the movie, *Avatar*. The only difference was that he was broader, had long dreadlocks and scales with reptile skin. I was fascinated with the movie when I was a little girl. Who would've thought I was able to see a better world—with a better mate.

**********

"This is Jewel's house? It looks haunted," Zambezi said when we swam on shore.

"It definitely looks different on the inside," Reef said.

There were clothes on a beach chair. The reef sisters always left their clothes out in case they didn't want to walk around naked after coming from the ocean. I grabbed a cardigan and Reef grabbed a long shirt. Zambezi's gold-plated shield covered his private areas but I still didn't want him walking around like that.

"Ummm, you can't go inside like that."

"What do you want me to? Put on girl clothes? There is nothing manly out here for me," he said.

I picked up a long-sleeve shirt and tied it around his waist backwards, so the longer part could cover his front. Reef fell out laughing because he was extremely pissed off.

"Ohhhh, I wish I had a camera," Reef said.

"Let's just hurry up," he replied.

Reef opened the door and the reef sisters were partying like always. The music was playing, and Darya walked around with a tray of sea wine. They were all naked and I was somewhat frustrated because Zambezi had an eye full of breasts and ass. I turned to see if he was looking and he turned his head.

"Can you all put some clothes on?"

"Why? We're home," Lake said.

"Can you have some respect for me? He's not single," I said. Rain and the rest of the sisters rushed upstairs to get some clothes. They were used to being free and I didn't fault them for that, but it was also about respect.

"Where is my father?" Zambezi asked.

"Upstairs on the left, it's the third door."

He kissed my cheek before going upstairs and Lake looked pissed off.

"Why is he here after what he said to me?" she asked.

"It's old and besides, you were disrespectful, too. If Rain and Reef aren't tripping anymore, then maybe you shouldn't! I'm starting to think you want him for yourself. You can have any man you want but it bothers you that you can't have him."

"Don't flatter yourself, little sister, I like my men rich. Not a poor fish-selling boy who lives in a small town like Oland," she said. Lake was drunk and probably high, too. She was a hard partier and she liked it so much, she worked at a club a few nights a week to dance naked. When we first met, we could talk about anything. I looked at her like a big sister, but something happened. Lake turned the music up louder and continued dancing. I walked away from her before I turned into the creature I hated the most and took her head off. Since I was at the mansion, I wanted to speak with Jewel about the dream I had of my mother and the man that was supposed to be my father. I also wanted to know if what Lesidi said about me was true. There seemed to be a lot of things that Jewel wasn't telling me. It was night time so that meant she was outside watching the ocean.

I left out the back door inside the kitchen and Jewel was lying in her beach chair. Her breasts were exposed, and her fish tail draped over the chair, covered in sand. She was combing her hair with a pearl and seashell comb.

"Something tells me you came here to ask me more questions," she said, looking at me.

"Why is everyone keeping secrets from me? It's like I'm expected to know everything, just because I'm some kind of water person. Who is my father? A girl came to me last night and told me I was part sea demon."

"I was expecting your mother to talk to you," Jewel said.

"My mother is gone. I think you all scared her away. You had Giva pretending to be a regular person who worked in town but the whole time, she was around to get me in the water. You all had this planned out. The cabin I'm staying in, you used to live in and never said anything. I'm sick of the lies. You sent for me so it's your responsibility to tell me about my parents."

Jewel took a sip from her sea wine cup while staring out into the ocean.

"Okay, Shore. Have a seat. I'm only telling you things that I'm certain of," she said while sitting up. I sat across from her, waiting to finally hear the truth.

"Around twenty years ago, we discovered Lake Deep. We went there because of the leaf shaped rock. Each water has a big special rock at the bottom because of Oceana. She marked them for us. When the young water fairies are born from the core of each waters, they go to the golden rock to wait for Oceana then she'll guide them back to the sea. Some would stay, and some would leave with her, but since Oceana was gone, I had to do what she used to do. So, I spent years traveling to her marked spots. One day, I came to Lake Deep and while I was swimming, I saw a familiar creature eating an animal. I knew then it was Caspian because I'll never forget his eyes. So, let's just say the sparks were flying. That same day, he took me into his cabin and made love to me. At that time, I just knew he really loved me, because he treated me so well and when I got pregnant, we were happy. I was helping him at the market, so I took Giva and Pearl with me. Lake Deep was our new home. But then there was a new face in town and she was very beautiful; her name was Adwoa. Caspian always had a weak spot for a beautiful face. He bedded her while I was pregnant and the day I gave birth, he left me. I knew something was off about Caspian. He was never an evil being, despite his mistakes. His eyes weren't the same, they were empty. I remember your mother telling me your father had empty eyes when he tried to kill her. She said he was cursed by a sea demon. At that time, I didn't think they existed until you brought Caspian here. A demon turned him that way. So, I don't know if your father was a demon but my experiences with

Caspian led me to believe maybe your mother was right about your father. That's all I know," Jewel said.

"I was so happy when I first met you all because I finally had a family and girls I could hang out with, but I hate myself knowing that I'm a part of an evil world. I don't feel the same. I'm constantly fighting with myself. I don't deserve the locket."

"You don't choose the locket, it chooses you. Listen to me and listen very carefully. That locket sees something inside of you that nobody else does. So what if you're a sea demon, we all have a wicked side. No creature is perfect, not even the gods we worship because they made mistakes, too. You're a princess and it'll take time to learn everything, but it will come. Just let the locket guide you," she said.

"Thank you very much. I needed to hear this."

I hugged my aunt Jewel and then the locket opened. Jewel disappeared, and the beach turned into a cave with pure green water.

"Is this the cave me and Zambezi came to?" I asked aloud. I hid behind a rock when a water fairy with an orange and purple tail glided underwater as small fish followed her. She pulled herself up from the water and sat on the edge, leaving her tail in for the fish to clean. I noticed she was wearing my locket.

"Who are you?" I asked but she didn't hear me. To my understanding, Oceana was the only goddess who wore the locket. The water fairy hummed the same song as Jewel and the rest of the reef sisters. I walked closer to her to see if I knew her from somewhere, but my mind was blank. Her fairy eyes turned black and I was more confused than ever. Her complexion turned gray and her white hair was thinned.

"SHORE!" Jewel said, and the cave disappeared. I was back to reality, sitting on the beach with Jewel.

"Huh?"

"What did you see?" Jewel asked.

"A water fairy that had this locket before my mother. I thought you said my mother was a goddess."

"She is one. The sea chose her. Did the fairy have orange hair?" Jewel asked.

"Yes."

"That's our elder sister, Elonora. She disappeared, and the locket was left behind. This happened a thousand years ago. I was very young and so was your mother. I barely remember her," Jewel said.

There was a crashing noise followed by screams and yelling coming from inside the mansion. I went inside and Jewel followed me. In the middle of the hallway stood about twenty sea demons. One of them being Laguna.

*What is going on?*

"How did you get here?" I asked.

"Well, let's just say a friend showed us the way," Laguna said. Nerida and his other brothers stepped through the crowd of sea demons.

"I told you to come with me, Shore. That's all you had to do and now you're stuck in the middle of a war.  Adwoa wants the locket, so give it here before it gets ugly," Nerida said.

"You're the reason why they're here! This is our home, Shore! Look what you have done!" Lake said.

Two sea dragons burst through the windows of Jewel's home. The bigger dragon snatched me up with his tail and tossed me onto his back. It was Zambezi. Half of Jewel's home collapsed because of the impact. Everyone ran from the house while it was falling. My reef sisters made it out but some of the sea demons and Nerida's brothers got caught by the debris.  A big wave came up and flooded the beach, knocking me off of Zambezi's back. All of us ended up in the ocean. A sea demon swam past us and snatched the necklace from around my neck while a gang of sea demons attacked Zambezi. A high-pitched siren noise came from my throat, knocking the sea demons off of Zambezi. He swam above me, his long tail with a sharp clasp at the end, piercing through the sea demons' skulls, instantly killing them. While swimming towards Zambezi, someone grabbed my hair.

*I know you killed my sister!* Laguna thought.

*I slit her throat and I'm going to do the same for you!*

*You took Zambezi away from me!* she said while we fought each other.

*I took what's mine!*

I bit Laguna's arm while swimming in circles, so I could rip it off. Sharp teeth burst through my gums, almost causing my skull to explode. My feet disappeared and were replaced by scaly legs with fins as feet. Horns ripped through my shoulders and went into Laguna's chest. Her blood clouded my vision as it covered us. A sea demon came to help Laguna and my locket made it explode.

*Sea demons don't kill each other!* Laguna thought.

A few demons attacked me from behind, pulling me away from Laguna so she could escape, but half her arm was stuffed between my teeth. The demons pulled me further into the ocean and a thunderstorm lightning bolt lit up the water, killing many demons near the surface. I had a feeling it came Zambezi because half his body was out of the water. The demons were scratching and clawing at me from behind. There were so many of them, I was struggling to fight them off. Jewel swam into us at high-speed like a torpedo. The impact knocked the sea demons off me. I was badly injured and could feel the flesh hanging off my back. My legs were terribly bitten to where I couldn't move them. I fell into Jewel and she wrapped her arms around me.

*Sea demons don't heal like us, Shore. Turn into a water fairy or you'll die. Please, just do it! I can't lose you like I lost my sisters. Turn back!*

Zambezi swam to us and wrapped his body around me and Jewel. His snout poked at me to keep me from passing out.

*Drink my blood, Shore! Do it now!*

Jewel pressed my face against Zambezi's neck and told me to drink his blood. I was getting weaker and couldn't keep my eyes opened. Zambezi turned into his human-like water form. His locs wrapped around me as he swam towards the surface. My vision was getting blurry, but I could make out all the dead bodies floating around. My reef sisters were still fighting the demons that were left. Bay was swimming underneath them to protect them from being attacked from below. Once we made it up to the top, I heard myself gasping for air. Zambezi bit his arm, drawing blood. He forced me to drink his blood by choking me, so I could open my mouth to breathe. Once my mouth opened, blood dripped to the back of my throat. His blood was sweet and tangy, even gave me a high feeling mixed with arousal.

*Noooo! I didn't want it. It's going to make me do what Adwoa did to Caspian.*

"I don't care about that. This is what your mother wanted from me. She knew what you were before you were born. She gave me to you, so I can heal you when you get like this and protect you through the waters. You need me the same way I need you," he said. He pressed his arm against my lips and I took more of his blood. I felt normal again and the sea demon faded away. Suddenly, Zambezi's necklace beamed and so did my locket as they clasped together. The sea demons sprouted into the air from the ocean, and were being evaporated. The lightning from the sky struck them, turning them to ash.

My reef sisters and Jewel came above the surface, looking around.

"The sea demons are gone but the male fairies got away. I'm going to hunt each one down and slaughter them for betraying their kind!" Jewel said.

"What happened? I was kicking ass in shark mode. Soon as I went in for the kill, the sea demon was pulled out the water," Reef said, smacking her hand against the water. She was mad.

"How is she one of them and us?" Darya asked.

"It doesn't matter, she's still family. We have bigger things to worry about like our home. My pool room is gone," Jewel said.

"Y'all can crash at my beach house," Zambezi said.

"Well, let's go," Rain said.

Since I was still somewhat weak, Zambezi swam with me wrapped in his arms. Bay and the rest of the fairies followed Zambezi while he guided them through the water.

*How did you and Bay know we were in trouble?*

*When I went upstairs to my father's bedroom, he wasn't inside. Bay said Father had been missing since this morning. So, we left the mansion and went into the ocean to see if he was there. When we came back after searching for him, we saw the sea demons on the beach,* he replied.

*Caspian must be in Oland.*

*Maybe so but at least he's better,* he said.

I snuggled against his chest and closed my eyes while we traveled through the bottom of the ocean to his beach house.

**\*\*\*\*\*\*\*\*\*\***

"This is sorta small," Lake said, looking around Zambezi's beach house.

"We love it, Zam. We didn't use much of the mansion anyway and I like the view since the house is near a cliff," Rain said.

"I appreciate it," Jewel said.

"Us, too," Reef and Darya said.

"Where is Giva?" I asked.

"My mother is never home," Reef said.

"She left hours ago before the fight. She said she had important business," Rain said.

"I feel like I'm living in an oyster," Lake said.

"You can leave! Zambezi gave you his home and you're bitching about nothing! We were just near-death moments ago and you still have the energy to be whining, bitch? You're a miserable whore!" I said.

"Yeah, you can bounce if you don't like it here," Bay said to Lake.

"Or you can always pick up more hours at the club to get a better house then there is the ocean, sea, lake and river to live in, too," Rain said.

"Child, be grateful!" Jewel said.

"I feel bad for this. Didn't you get this house to get away from Oland?" Rain asked.

"Yeah, but I'm staying with Shore," Zambezi said, and everyone said, "Awwwww."

"I'll see you all in a few days," I said.

"Okay, give us all a hug," Rain said. I hugged everyone but Lake. Jewel walked me and Zambezi to the sliding doors of the living room. We were going back to the Ocean to get to Oland.

"You two be safe and remember what I told you. You don't choose it, it chooses you," she said. While I hugged her again, I whispered in her ear.

"Tell Bay the truth."

"I will when I get over the fear but right now he looks at me like an older sister. I'm satisfied with that," she whispered back. I pulled away from her and she went back into the house.

"Bay, you coming?" Zambezi asked.

"Naw, I'll be back home tomorrow," he said, putting his arm around Rain.

"Be safe," Zambezi said.

Jewel closed the door and it was just me and Zambezi. He looked down at me while grabbing my hand.

"Let's spend the night at the cave," he said.

"Last one there is a rotten egg," I said.

I ran towards the cliff, but Zambezi leaped over my head and dived into the ocean before me. When my body hit the water, my tail emerged.

*Cheater!*

*Naw, I'm just a better swimmer. Keep up, beautiful, the loser has to work at the market by themselves tomorrow.*

My fish tail pushed harder through the water while following Zambezi. Once I caught up to him, I wrapped my arms around his neck and wrestled with him.

*Get off me, demon!* he said.

*Not funny, alligator!*

He pulled me off his back, so I could face him. He moved my hair away from my face.

*When I saw your wounded body, I got scared thinking I was going to lose you. At that moment, I knew then I couldn't live without you because I love you,* he said.

If we weren't underwater, he would've seen my happy tears.

*I love you, too. From the moment you tried to get me away from Jewel at the bottom of Lake Deep.*

Zambezi pressed his lips against mine and I grabbed a hold of his shoulders while our bodies intertwined. Moments later, he pulled away from me and took off, gliding through the water.

*I'm serious about this competition. You better catch up or else you're going to be serving raw fish tomorrow!* he said.

*I'm going to get you, asshole!*

Even though Adwoa and her clan was still out there somewhere, hiding in the swamp, she was no longer a threat to me—to us. No matter what she did, she couldn't get my locket. But hopefully, one day, I'd find her. In the meantime, I was enjoying my new love life with my handsome mate.

# Oceana

**The next day...**

"Okay, Oceana. Today is your day to swim. We've been waiting long enough," Giva said. I was standing on the edge of a dock, looking at the ducks playing in the water. Although my memory was back, I still hadn't returned to the waters.

"I don't think I can do it, Giva!" I said.

"We've talked about this, now jump!" Giva said from behind me.

"I don't think I can do it! You said Shore is coming into herself now. Maybe she doesn't need me!" I said, staring at the water.

"Shore needs to know things that only you know!" Giva yelled at me.

The water seemed to get higher and I stepped away from it.

"Please forgive me for this," Giva said.

She wrapped her arms around me then jumped into the water. She pulled me underneath while my arms flailed. Giva pulled me further down towards the river's bed which meant the bottom where the rocks rested.

*Focus, Oceana! You know what to do! Feel the waters welcoming you. They are talking to you,* Giva said.

The fish rushed towards me. They swam through my hair and between my legs. The feeling was so familiar that I cried.

*My babies. Come!*

There were hundreds of fish covering my body.

*They're embracing you, Oceana. See, this is still your real home,* Giva said.

My hair began changing. Its once black color was now jet-black with gold streaks and gold starfish were at the tips of my ends.

*Look, Giva! My tail!*

My tail was covered in gold with black sparkling scales. I didn't realize how much I missed my gold nails until they returned. The fish gathered underneath and pushed me upwards towards the surface. My body soared through the water like a dolphin before diving back into the water.

*I feel so happy and energetic. I was starting to get arthritis in my hands from busing tables.*

*A queen's riches are in the waters, not in a human's restaurant,* she said. I hugged Giva and pulled her close to me.

*Take me to Shore. I want to see her.*

Giva grabbed my hand and guided me through the Ocean. I missed Shore very much. It had been a month since I'd seen her.

## Oland...

I pulled myself up on the rock in front of the cabin. The land was quiet, and the cabin looked different because it was remodeled.

"I don't think Shore is home. I don't hear her. It's day time and usually she's outside."

"Shore works at the market with Zambezi. She'll be back, but I have to head home. I'll return in a few days to take you to see Jewel. She'll be happy to see you," Giva said. She blew me a kiss before diving under. I sniffed the air and there was a familiar scent.

"Oceana?" a voice said. The girl was sitting in the grass peeling corn. She had a young face with very long braids. My tail disappeared, and I was able to walk. The girl backed away from me, she was frightened.

"YOU!" I yelled at her.

"Please, let me explain!" she cried.

"You're the one that killed my sister! It was you! Where is my daughter?"

"She and Zambezi are spending the day together. I come here to use the water for my corn. Please, don't kill me. Adwoa made me do it. I regret it, but I had to do it or else Adwoa would've sent all of her children to kill me," she said. I picked her up by the hair and she kicked and screamed.

"Take me to Adwoa!"

"It's too many," she said.

"Take me to Adwoa or I'll kill you!" I said.

"I'll do it! Please, stop hurting me," she replied. I let her go and she fell onto the ground.

"Adwoa is in a swamp, but it's dangerous for your kind," she said.

"Adwoa needs to die. You all thought I wasn't going to come back to the waters?"

"Yes, we did because you've been gone for many years," she said.

"What is your name?"

"Lesidi," she said.

"Let's go!"

Lesidi stared at me in disbelief. "You want to walk through Oland without any clothes on?" she asked. I grabbed a dirty long T-shirt off a tree stomp then pulled it over my head.

"Now, go!"

I followed her through the woods to get on the main dirt road to the town of Oland.

"Are you going to kill me? I'm very sorry for what I did," she said.

"Adwoa has made many of you hurt us. I know she made you do it, but it still doesn't change that you did."

"Shore is one of us," she said.

"Don't worry about my daughter because there is still some good inside her. I can't say the same for you all."

Lesidi walked with her head down, she was still ashamed. She looked younger than Shore, which meant she was cursed at a young age.

Adwoa was probably the only thing she had for a mother.

"Are you friends with my daughter?"

"She doesn't like me very much, but I understand why she doesn't. Hopefully I can be her friend one day."

"How long is this walk?"

"I don't know but it's long. It will be night time by the time we get there," she said.

*Adwoa is the reason why I had to kill Shore's father and she has to be punished.*

\*\*\*\*\*\*\*\*\*\*

It was night time when we made it to Adwoa's swamp. The green thick water had a stench and it reeked of death. I almost gagged from the smell and the mud was thick enough to swallow me. It wasn't a good environment for the fairies, it was hard to breathe, almost as if someone had their hand over my nose.

"I'll stay here and wait for you. The ship is a ways from here. You won't miss it," Lesidi said.

I followed the direction Lesidi pointed me to. Animal and human bones were scattered everywhere. Adwoa's swamp was located deep into the woods after you passed Oland; it was deserted, perhaps lost land. I walked through the mushy water until I saw a broken ship with fungus growing over it. The place was also gloomy, and the trees didn't have any leaves. The land was dead.

I grabbed a hold of the edge of the ship and pulled myself up. Old rusty chains were embedded into the wall of the ship. I heard voices coming from the upper-deck. It was a man and a woman arguing. A loud squeak from the rat I stepped on by accident echoed throughout the ship.

"Someone is here!" a woman said. I heard heavy footsteps coming from the upper-level. A young man with long hair came down the stairs. He froze when he saw me then ran back upstairs. I followed him, and the stairs led me to the main level of the ship. Adwoa was sitting in her chair, half of her face was normal, and the other half was of a monster.

"Oceana, Oceana. You finally found your way back to the waters. You should've stayed out of it. My business isn't with you anymore, it's with your daughter because she has what I want. But now it's very personal since her and her sisters killed my children. I have no one left!" Adwoa yelled. The fish in the bowl next to her were angelfish. They looked like Shore's fish.

"You stole my daughter's fish?"

"Yes, and the female fish is laying eggs, waiting for the male to fertilize them. Looks like Shore wants to get pregnant or is pregnant. Once the eggs hatch, I will kill them all. Tell Shore I'll spare her unborn child if she hands over the locket. Elonora won't stop until I have what belongs to her," Adwoa said.

"Elonora?"

"Yes, my goddess," Adwoa said.

"She was once a fairy! Stop your lies! I will never believe she was responsible for this!"

"No lie is being started. I'm one of her children," Adwoa said. There was a creaking noise behind me and I turned around to a familiar face.

"My sweet mate. How did you find me? Seems like everyone is coming to join the party," Adwoa smiled.

"I found him at his market when I went to Oland and told me him everything! End this now, Adwoa. I can't find Laguna and I know Ara is dead," a woman with Caspian said.

"Cascade, what are you doing in here, son?" Caspian asked the young man next to Adwoa.

"He's with me, no need to speak to him. Glad to see you being a man again," Adwoa said to Caspian. Caspian charged into Adwoa and grabbed her by the throat. The young man, Cascade, stuck his nails into Caspian's neck. I grabbed Shore's fish and swallowed them to keep them safe. Adwoa's screams filled the ship while Caspian ripped her throat apart. Cascade's strength was no match for Caspian.

"Die, bitch! Just die!" Caspian yelled.

"Stay out of it, Cascade! He's freeing us from her!" a woman said.

"I love her, Katana!" Cascade sobbed. Adwoa's dead body fell on the floor and Caspian grabbed Cascade by the throat and slammed him into the ship.

"You were my son's friend and you betrayed him!" Caspian said.

"No more than you betrayed him!" Cascade said. Caspian sank his teeth into Cascade's neck and ripped his throat out. Blood dripped from his sharp teeth, making him appear even more menacing. He took his fist and slammed it into the ship, making it collapse. I rushed off, falling into the water before the debris fell on top of me. Caspian helped me out of the thick water.

"I still dislike you very much, but I know you won't last another minute here," he said. The woman, Katana, fell off the ship, but a piece of sharp wood went into her stomach then the rest collapsed on top of her.

"Katana deserved it even though she helped me find Adwoa," Caspian said.

"And you deserve the same fate."

"Tell my sons I'm going back to the sea for a while. I'll be back in a few months. I need to feel like myself again, so I can be a better father. I lost myself," he admitted.

"I wish you all the luck."

Lesidi ran to me when we got halfway out the swamp. Caspian went his separate way.

"Is she dead?" Lesidi asked.

"Caspian killed her."

Lesidi helped me out of the swamp.

"I'm not going to kill you, but I don't want to ever see you again. I still can't forget you killing Harbor."

"Thank you very much, Oceana."

***********

Shore and Zambezi were playing around in the water when I made it back to the cabin.

"SHORE!" I called out.

I jogged towards the lake and she was swimming towards the land. When she got out, she jumped into my arms.

"I missed you!" she said. I kissed her face before squeezing her tighter.

"Adwoa won't bother anyone anymore. Caspian killed her."

"You saw my father? We can't find him," Zambezi said while walking out the lake.

"He left but he's coming back. Give him time to find himself. Adwoa really messed him up," I replied.

"I love this hair, Ma. I'm so happy you left. I thought you were homeless, living on the street with an empty soup can, begging for change for a beer," Shore said, wiping her eyes.

"Go inside the cabin and bring me a bowl. Adwoa had your fish in her ship," I told Shore. She ran to the cabin, giving me time to speak with Zambezi.

"Your friend Cascade was one of those things. He was there with Adwoa. I'm just letting you know because your father said you two were friends but he's dead."

"He was here one day but we thought Lesidi stole Shore's fish. That's messed up, but we weren't cool like that. We just went to club together, but Shore told me about you and my mother. She saw it through her locket. I just want to thank you for picking me for your daughter," he smiled. Zambezi was very charming; no wonder Shore fell for him the first time she saw him. Shore came out of the cabin with a bowl. She went to the lake and filled it up with water. I pulled the fish out of my mouth and dropped them into the bowl.

"I'll be inside the cabin," Zambezi said while taking the fish from Shore.

"Do I give this back?" Shore asked about the locket.

"No, it's yours."

"Come, Ma. Swim with me," Shore said, pulling me into the water. Once the water was deep enough, we dived under, swimming together. I'll never leave the waters or neglect my reef family—ever again.

# Laguna

My head was throbbing, my mouth was dry, and I could barely breathe. I swatted vultures away from my arm that Shore mauled. After the fight and storm, my body washed up near an old factory. I was dying. The rage I had for Shore was keeping me alive. I wanted to kill her for killing my sister and taking Zambezi away from me. Adwoa came to me and promised that she could make me beautiful in a way where Zambezi wouldn't notice Shore, but all she did was turn me into a monster.

"Arrghhhhh!" I screamed out in pain because my legs were broken.

"SOMEONE HELP ME!" I cried.

A figure appeared in front of me, but my vision was damaged. My eyes were swollen from the fight.

"My child, my child," the voice said.

"Who are you?"

"You called for help," the voice said.

"Please help me, I'm dying," I begged.

"If I help you, what can you do for me?" she asked.

"Whatever you want. Please, just get me away from the vultures who are watching me die so they can eat me."

"I can heal you, but I want you to be my vessel. I need Shore's locket and you can get the revenge you want for her. Just tell me you accept my help and I'll give you what you want," she said.

"I'll do anything you want me to do."

"My gift will come soon. Don't fail me the same way Adwoa failed me. She got weak, but you will be a better vessel for me. You're young and fresh," she said then disappeared.

*I'll do better than Adwoa. I promise, my mother...*

**Finale coming soon...**

9 781689 441964